Also by Michelle Gordon:

Fiction:

Earth Angel Series:

The Earth Angel Training Academy

The Earth Angel Awakening

The Other Side

Visionary Collection

Heaven dot com

The Doorway to PAM

The Elphite

Non-fiction:

Choose Your Own Reality

Oracle Cards:

Aria's Oracle

Velvet's Oracle

Amethyst's Oracle

I'm Here

Michelle Gordon

www.theamethystangel.com

First published in Great Britain in 2014 by The Amethyst Angel

Copyright © 2014 by Michelle Gordon
Cover Artwork by madappledesigns copyright © madappledesigns

ISBN: 978-1499601107

The moral right of the author has been asserted.

Book mentioned:
Infinite You by Pamala Oslie
lifecolorscity.com

First Edition

Acknowledgements

I have decided to write my thank you messages entirely in Haikus, enjoy!

Jon Fellows:
My inspiration,
My twin flame, my sweet true love,
I am yours, always.

Liz Gordon:
You're a creative
Genius, my sister, and
An amazing friend.

Sally Byrne:
Belief and support
In abundance you supply
Deepest gratitude.

Elizabeth Lockwood:
Your time, your patience,
Your love, your friendship, your help
Mean the world to me.

Niki & Dan:
Your wonderful and
Crazy madness is what makes
It all possible.

Liz Chukwu
Your light shines so bright,
That you make possible what
Seems impossible.

*Everyone who has ever loved me,
supported me, and cheered me on:*
I am blessed to have
You in my life. I'm thankful
Every day for you.

This book is for Nathan, who persistently haunted me until I finally wrote it.

Chapter One

"Hello?"

I sat up, breathing heavily. My eyes darted around the darkened room. Just seconds ago I had been enjoying a dream about going on holiday to New York, when I felt something touch my hair, waking me up suddenly. But aside from my breathing, the room was silent. I lay back down, and pulled the covers up a bit higher. I tried to close my eyes and go back to sleep, but the feeling that someone was there wouldn't go away.

"Who's there? What do you want?"

Silence. There was no answer to my whisper.

I breathed in deeply and squeezed my eyes shut. *Got an early morning tomorrow*, I thought to myself. *Really need to get enough sleep.* Before I could mentally go over my to-do list, I had blissfully slipped off to sleep again.

* * *

"Marielle? Earth to Marielle?"

The fingers snapping in front of my face finally caught my attention and I looked up from my soggy bowl of cornflakes.

"What?" I asked, before standing up and taking my bowl to the sink.

"Are you okay? I asked you four times whether you had

your creative writing class today."

I blinked at Sarah. "Yes, at two this afternoon. I have politics this morning. Why?" I ran the tap and rinsed the bowl out. I couldn't seem to concentrate. My sudden awakening last night had really unsettled me. It was the fourth time in a week I'd woken up suddenly, feeling as though someone was touching my hair or my face. Surely that wasn't normal?

"You're doing it again," Sarah said.

I re-focused and tried to give her my full attention. "I'm sorry, I'm a little spaced out this morning. Didn't sleep very well. What did you say?"

"I was asking if you wanted to go to the talk this evening, in the Black Swan Bookshop."

"What's it about?"

"I think it's about hypnosis, they have a guest speaker. It starts at six."

I shrugged. "Why not? I don't have any other plans." I glanced up at the clock. "Shit, going to be late for class." I put the bowl on the drying rack, and headed back to my room. At least living on campus meant that most of my classes were less than a ten minute walk away. My politics lecturer was pretty laid back anyway, he wasn't normally bothered when people were late.

It was only October, but it was already freezing. I layered up and headed outside, pleased that for once, it wasn't raining. Within minutes, I reached the English block. It was an ugly building. Why on earth people were allowed to design and build such monstrosities in the seventies was anyone's guess. At least it was nice and warm inside. Once seated in class, I got my pens and notebook out, and set them out neatly on the desk in front of me. A few others came in after me, and Mr Hinchley started his lecture.

I wasn't overly keen on the politics classes, but they were compulsory for my degree, so I was putting up with them. I tried to keep track of Hinchley's words, making notes of his most important points, but my mind kept wandering.

"Marielle? Do you have any thoughts on the subject?" Caught out for the second (or was it third?), time that morning, I stared blankly at the lecturer.

"No," I said honestly. "I don't."

A couple of my classmates laughed and Hinchley shook his head, a hint of a smile on his face. "Very well, perhaps if you pay attention to the next part you may have some thoughts on it."

I nodded, my cheeks heating up. I lowered my head and tried to look like I was taking detailed notes. But a few words on the page stopped me.

I was with you last night.

I frowned. It was my handwriting, but I must have written it while I was staring out of the window, my mind elsewhere. What did it mean? Why had I written that?

I wrenched my gaze from the words and forced myself to pay attention to the last twenty minutes of the lecture. But as I left the room, I could honestly say that not a single word had entered my memory.

Somehow, I found myself back in the dorm kitchen, holding a mug of tea, but had no real idea of how I got there.

I knew I should start paying more attention, and not get so lost in my thoughts all the time. Otherwise I could end up missing months, if not years of my life. I really didn't want to wake up one day and realise I'd been sleepwalking through what were supposed to be the best years of my life.

"You're in another world again aren't you?"

I looked up and smiled at Sarah. "Yes. I don't know if it's the lack of decent sleep or what, but I just seem to be out of it at the moment."

Sarah frowned and flicked the kettle back on. "Perhaps we might learn something tonight that will help. Maybe you need to ground yourself."

"Ground myself? Sounds painful."

Sarah laughed. "It's not. It just means connecting to the earth. Rather than floating around, disconnected."

I nodded. "Sounds good. How do I do that?"

"I just imagine there are roots coming from the bottom of my feet into the ground, and they're anchoring me, securing me."

"I've always wanted to be a tree," I joked.

Sarah shook her head. "Ha ha," she said sarcastically. "Just try it. See if it keeps you in this world for more than five minutes."

"I will. Do I need to be barefoot outside or anything?"

"No, not really. Just stand or sit with both feet firmly on the ground and visualise the roots." She picked up the mug of tea she had just made. "Now I have to do my essay before I'm allowed out to play tonight. I'll see you in here at quarter to six?"

"A whole essay? In one afternoon? That's impressive."

"Don't be silly, you know how long it takes me to write them. I'm just in the planning stages right now, but I need a clear structure done today, so I can start the research." She waved and left the kitchen, leaving me to stare into my mug of tea. I set the mug down and closed my eyes. I breathed in deeply and imagined tree roots extending from the soles of my feet, through the lino, through the foundations of the building, and into the earth, deep down below. I breathed in deeply again, and opened my eyes. Everything looked a little clearer, a little more real. I felt awake.

I finished my tea and went to do some reading before my creative writing class.

*   *   *

"The exercise for today is to just write anything that comes to mind, for thirty minutes. A stream of consciousness. It doesn't need to make sense, or tell a story or anything. Just whatever thoughts come up, write them down."

My creative writing professor, a published author himself, handed out some sheets of paper with the instructions on, then went back to his desk. He tapped his watch. "Thirty minutes. Then we'll read some of them out."

I skimmed over the instructions, and put the nib of my pen to the first line on the page of my notebook. What was I thinking?

Do you know that moment, between asleep and awake? That moment where you hover between two worlds? The one of life and the one of dreams? That is where I am.

I am there, in that gap, in that moment, in that place that doesn't exist. I am there in the silence, I am there, and I am here, and I am nowhere.

But if you were to know this, if you were to speak my name, I would no longer hover in the in between, I would be by your side. I would protect you, and care for you, in a way that only I could.

The question is, do you believe that?

Chapter Two

I watch her read the words. I watch her face as she tries to figure out what they mean. It feels like it took some effort to write my words through her, to influence her mind. And yet, it took no effort at all. Because I do not exist in a relative world. There is no good or bad here. No hot or cold, no up or down. Everything here just simply is. Or is not. Or both.

It took a fair bit of adjustment. To get used to this world. I have no form. I just am.

I figured, that if I still existed in some form when I died, I would move on. I would see my family who had passed on, I would maybe have a life review, and I would get to choose a new life or go forward. I don't know where to, but just, forward. But it didn't happen in that way. I don't know why. I guess I chose not to move on. I chose not to pick a new form. I chose to stay in this state. But I don't remember making that decision.

As I watch her now, it seems clear to me that I am supposed to have more of a presence in her life. Which is funny really, because right now, that's all I can be to her. A presence. A spiritual presence.

It seems weird to label things. Funny. Sad. Past. Present. Weird. None of it really has any meaning to me anymore. But I know it means something to her, and that's what keeps me trying to get through to her. She senses me, I know she does. And not because I can read her mind, because I can't. But I can see in her eyes that she knows when I am around. That I am trying to get through. That I am trying to help her.

I watch her read my words for the fourth time, when the professor calls on her to read them aloud. She looks up at him, and I see the fear in her eyes. He doesn't believe in anything spiritual. I can sense that about him. And she knows it too.

"I'm not sure I want to," she says.

"Why not?"

"Because it's, well, weird. I don't know where it came from."

It came from me, I whisper.

"Read it anyway." Her professor lacks any kind of intuition. If he had any empathy at all he wouldn't make her read it.

She stutters over some of the words, but she manages to read it out loud. And again I marvel at how I have managed to get her such a clear message. Surely she will recognise it is me?

I notice that when she finishes reading, a tear falls and hits the word 'believe', smudging the ink on the paper.

Her emotion intrigues me. Does she realise it is me? Or do the words just invoke a longing within her, as she has yet to meet anyone who would care for and protect her?

When I arrived here, and began to watch her, it amazed me she was still single. We had not spoken in real life for a good few years before I died. And even then it had been mere pleasantries exchanged between two people who had once gone to school with one another, but weren't close friends.

I imagined that by now she would have a boyfriend, that she would have found someone who deserved her, who loved her with everything he had. But it seemed like she wasn't even dating. How could that be?

She seems to be moving in slow motion after her class, closing her notebook carefully and putting it in her bag. It will be interesting to watch what happens later in the hypnosis event. I will be there, waiting to see if there is a way to contact her.

I have tried to communicate with her every night for the past week, but just as I am about to reach her mind, she senses my energy in reality, and it jolts her awake. I hate to see the fear on her face, and hear her heart pumping as she tries to work out what is happening.

Every time she whispers – 'Who's there?' I reply:
"It's me. It's Nathan."

*   *   *

How had I let myself become the volunteer? One minute I was sat in the small audience, and the next I was sat in front of the audience, about to be the hypnotised guinea pig.

I looked down at my traitor hand, the hand that had shot up in the air when a volunteer was called for. My cheeks were burning at the thought that not only was everyone watching me, but that I might end up doing ridiculous things with no recollection of them afterwards.

"Now, just close your eyes, and listen to my voice. I'm going to count down from ten, and when I reach one, you will be relaxed, and open to my suggestions."

His voice was really quite melodic and relaxing. I closed my eyes, happy to shut out all of the people watching me. He continued to speak, then he began to count down.

I could remember him saying 'four' but after that, something strange happened. Suddenly I was no longer in the Black Swan Bookshop but in school again, sitting in GSCE Media Studies, listening to my teacher talking about how we were going to create our own rock band.

I looked around, and all of my classmates were listening intently, unaware anything was amiss. I tried to recall this moment from my past, but my memories of my teenage years were extremely hazy. And I had forgotten (or blocked out?) most of my school days.

As I looked back at my teacher, one of the boys caught my eye. He smiled. Surprised, I smiled back. Though I'd actually had a crush on him for a while, I didn't think he knew I existed. After all, he had a steady girlfriend.

He kept my gaze for a few more moments, and my smile slipped from my face. Did he know I was visiting this moment from the future?

He looked back at the teacher and seemed to carry on writing notes. I looked down at my own notebook.

Remember this.

I read the words, written in my own handwriting, and pondered their significance. Why had I come back to this moment? Why was it important?

I couldn't explain how I came to be back in the bookshop again. One moment I was in my classroom at school, the next, it had faded and suddenly I was back in the limelight again. I blinked and looked up at the hypnotist, who was peering at me, looking concerned.

"Are you okay?" he asked.

I nodded. "Uh, yeah, what happened?"

"Nothing. I finished counting, and it was like you were asleep. You were completely impervious to my suggestions. So I woke you back up again."

"Oh." My cheeks were burning again. "Sorry. I guess I'm not a very good subject for hypnosis. Maybe someone else should try." I jumped up and returned to my seat next to Sarah.

"You okay?" she whispered.

"I'll tell you later," I whispered back.

The rest of the evening was a blur, and instead of the hypnotist, all I could see was my old classroom, those words and his smile.

On the way back to the dorm, we stopped at the chippy and bought dinner. We filled the kitchen with the greasy smell of chip fat, and ate off of plates with a fork, which was not a very student-like thing to do – it created washing up for a start – but Sarah and I weren't like typical students in many ways.

"So what happened?"

I shrugged. "I'm not sure, I seemed to slip into a memory."

"A memory? So the hypnosis worked?"

"Did he suggest I return to a moment in my past? I don't remember anything he said."

"No, he just counted down from ten, then it was like you were in a coma. He asked you questions and you just didn't respond. It was a little bit freaky, actually."

"I was in school again. In Media Studies class in year eleven."

"How strange," Sarah said, dipping a chip in ketchup. "Did anything happen?"

I shook my head. "Not really. No one really noticed anything. Except, there was this guy..."

"Oh yeah? What guy?"

"He was just a guy in my year, we only shared one class. I didn't really know him, but I kind of had a crush on him. And in this memory, vision, whatever, he turned and smiled at me."

"That's it?"

"Yeah, then he looked away and then I woke up."

"Do you think it means anything?" Sarah asked, sipping her water.

"Like what? I hardly knew the guy."

"Maybe you're supposed to contact him. Sometimes when you dream about someone, or think of them out of the blue, it's because you're supposed to speak to them."

I thought about it. All of the weird things that had been happening to me recently did seem to point to doing something, but none of it really made any sense. And why him? Why would he be coming into my mind now?

I ate two more chips then pushed my plate away. The smallest portion of chips was still too much for me to eat. "Well, if I am supposed to contact him, I'm sure there'll be a sign of some sort. I'll wait until then."

Sarah nodded. "Sounds fair. What are you doing this weekend? Do you want to come to the Union with me tomorrow night? It's fetish night."

I raised my eyebrows. "Fetish night? Really? Um, I don't know."

"Oh come on, it'll be fun. You don't have to dress up, just wear black, you'll be fine."

"I guess it could be good. I should go out more really. Is it normal for a twenty-one year old to just want to stay in with a good book or movie by herself?"

"I don't know if it's normal, but I don't think it's healthy. You should get out, mingle, and meet people. How many people do you know here outside of this dorm and your classes?"

"Um," I thought about it for a minute. I chatted to the porter the other day, I wondered if that counted. I saw the look on Sarah's face. Probably not. "None."

"Exactly. You're coming with me. I can do your make-up if you want."

"Okay, I guess." I stood up and went over to the bin. I

scraped the remnants of my chips into the bin then took the plate and fork to the sink. "What are you up to tomorrow?"

"My essay research. I was going to hole up in the library. You?"

"I need to borrow someone's notes from class this morning. I was so spaced out I pretty much missed the whole thing, and I'm sure he'll be expecting an essay on it, so I need to catch up." I dried my plate and fork and put them away in my cupboard. I filled a glass with water to take back to my room. "I'll see you tomorrow."

"Good night," Sarah called out as I left the kitchen.

Chapter Three

If it were possible for me to feel frustration, I think I would be feeling it very strongly right now. Another sign? Really? Have I not given her a million already? The notes, the words, the feeling of not being alone, and tonight, I manage to get that entire memory into her mind. Goodness, she is receptive to hypnosis. Her friend even tells her she needs to get in touch with me, and yet she still doesn't get it.

I don't get upset. Or sad, or angry. But after listening to their conversation, I am aware she doesn't know I have died. She has no idea I am no longer a living, breathing human. That I am now a spirit, an energy, just a leftover imprint of something that no longer exists in her world.

I run through the possibilities of her discovering the truth. Surely if she knows I am dead she might take the experiences of the last week more seriously?

Within a second, I leave her side, and I move to where her best friend from school is watching TV with her boyfriend.

I send energy toward her, the idea that she should write to Marielle. I send energy to her boyfriend, reminding him of my death, which I know he is aware of. We were all in the same year at school. I'd not really spoken to either of them much, but we all knew each other.

"I should really write to Marielle. I wonder how things

are going in university."

"Yeah, have you told her about Nathan?"

"Nathan? Did she know him?"

"I think so, didn't they have some classes together?"

Jane shrugs. "I guess so. I'll mention it. I'll write to her tomorrow."

"Okay."

I smile. I wonder if humans realise how many of their thoughts and conversations are influenced by the unseen energies that surround them. Do they have any idea that their 'random' thoughts are in fact placed there deliberately?

I move back to Marielle, and find her room darkened, her sleeping form tucked under the covers. It is difficult not to try and reach out to her. But I don't want to wake her; because of me, she hasn't been sleeping properly. But I don't need to try and reach her in her dreamstate now, because soon, Jane will write to her, and she will get her next sign.

I just have to be patient. Though I don't really know what impatience is anymore. I watch her eyelids flicker and wonder what she dreams of. Does she ever dream of me?

*   *   *

The world looked totally different after a decent night's sleep. My lectures actually made sense, and I took coherent notes that should be easy to turn into the required coursework.

But it felt like something was missing. Like I had forgotten something important.

I was simultaneously looking forward to and dreading the evening. Fetish night? Not normally my cup of tea, but I had to admit, it would make a change from the usual

Friday night movie, watched alone in my room.

It wasn't that I wanted to be a loner. It wasn't that I disliked company. I just preferred the quiet, I preferred just being myself. Around other people I found myself acting in whatever way seemed appropriate, rather than just being me.

I rummaged through my wardrobe for a suitable outfit for the evening. Sarah had insisted I could just wear black, but I figured she didn't mean a black top and jeans. I felt like I should at least attempt to enter into the spirit of the theme.

I found a black velvet camisole that was supposed to be a pyjama top and a short black skirt. Both were bought as part of previous fancy dress outfits. They were not my usual taste, I always wore jeans and t-shirts, with knitted cardigans or jumpers over the top in the winter. I rarely wore skirts and I never wore dresses.

I laid out the outfit, and shrugged. It still seemed fairly boring, but slightly more interesting than what I usually wore.

There were a few hours left until I had to get ready, so I sat on my bed and picked up the book I'd bought the night of the hypnotism evening. It was interesting, but my mind kept wandering. After five minutes of not taking in a single word on the page, I put the book down and lay back on my bed. I closed my eyes, and even though I had slept well the night before, found myself drifting off.

*   *   *

"Don't go."

I sat upright on the bed and looked around. My heart was pounding from my sudden awakening. The room was dark, the sun had long set. I switched on the bedside lamp and peered at my clock. Cursing, I got up and started stripping my clothes off.

"Marielle?" There was a knock at the door. "You ready for me to do your makeup?"

I went to the door and let Sarah in.

"You're still in your underwear?"

I shook my head. "I know, I just lay down for five minutes and fell asleep for three hours. It won't take me long to get ready though."

Sarah walked past me into my room and I took in her outfit. She was wearing a skin-tight black PVC catsuit that showed every curve. The outfit was completed by black stilettos, sultry makeup and bright red fingernails. I whistled. "Wow. That really does not leave much to the imagination."

She did a little twirl. "I know. Do you think I'll get any action tonight?"

"If you don't, every man there must be blind." I started pulling on my more humble black ensemble. "I, on the other hand, will be happily propping up the bar and people watching."

Sarah frowned. "I think I have some fishnet stockings if you want to borrow them. They'd liven up the outfit a bit. And I have a necklace that would look good on you."

I nodded. "Sure, why not?"

While Sarah went to her room to retrieve the tights and jewellery, I quickly finished dressing and straightened my hair.

"Here you go." Sarah handed me the stockings, and I slipped them on. I didn't own any high heels, so my black boots would have to do. I put the necklace on and looked at myself in the mirror. I looked like I was playing dressing up. I had no idea how women pulled off outfits like this seriously.

"Right. Now sit down while I put some makeup on you. You're as pale as a ghost anyway, so it shouldn't take me long."

The mention of ghosts reminded me of the voice that had woken me up. I had forgotten about it until that moment. I wondered what it meant by 'Don't go'. Did it mean I shouldn't go tonight?

"Keep still. If you keep fidgeting I'll end up poking you in the eye with the eyeliner."

"Sorry," I muttered, doing my best not to move my head or facial muscles.

After what seemed like hours, I was deemed fit to go out. I shoved my purse and some other essentials into a tiny black handbag and we headed out the door.

"Aren't you wearing a coat?" I asked, grabbing my long black wool coat from the hook on my door.

"Nah, I don't feel the cold, I'll be fine."

Shaking my head I followed her down the corridor and out of the building. We hadn't had any serious frosts yet, but the tarmacked paths still glittered in the lamplight as we made our way down the hill to the Student Union. She would never admit it, but I swear Sarah shivered all the way there. Even I felt a little chilly, wearing a skirt in October was never a particularly good idea, let alone a tiny skirt like I was wearing.

Ten minutes later, we reached the squat, ugly Student Union building and went inside. We were greeted with a very welcome blast of warmth. After paying to get in, we headed into the darkened main room. My eyes bugged out when I saw what people were wearing. It was clear that most of the outfits hadn't just been bought for this event, but were actually a part of their (secret) wardrobes.

The music wasn't particularly loud, but it pulsed and throbbed and seemed to fill every molecule of my body.

"I'll get the first round, what do you want?" Sarah asked, heading for the bar.

"Archers and lemonade, please." I figured if I was to make it through the evening, I would need some alcohol in me. Sarah nodded and I went to find us a table. I couldn't believe how packed it was, I'd only been to the Union a couple of times before, and it hadn't been anywhere near this busy. I managed to find a vacant table. I took my coat off and put it on the back of the chair. I was only sat there for a minute before I heard a voice right next to my ear.

"Hi, there, I don't think I've seen you before."

I turned toward the voice and found myself staring into a dark pair of eyes. I shook my head. "I don't come out very often."

He smiled, and I leaned back a little to take in the rest of his face. He wasn't bad looking, perhaps not really my taste, but still, not bad.

"What do you normally do?"

"Study, read, watch movies. Normal stuff."

He looked me up and down and raised an eyebrow. "Would have thought you'd have a more exciting life than that."

I could feel my cheeks heating up. If he thought I looked a little dangerous, he was going to love it when Sarah arrived. "I guess I just like having a quiet life." Ironically, the music suddenly got louder at that moment and I had to shout the last two words.

He chuckled and leaned in closer. "Can I get you a drink?"

I shook my head again and was just about to tell him Sarah was getting them when she arrived at the table. I watched his reaction when he saw her and I wasn't disappointed. His eyes nearly popped out of their sockets and he looked her up and down more times than was appropriate.

She sat down opposite me and handed me my drink. I took a sip, watching the guy to see what he would do next. Would he just move on to Sarah? I certainly couldn't blame him if he did, but it would confirm that he wasn't really worth talking to.

"Are you okay?" Sarah mouthed.

I nodded. To my surprise, the guy leaned toward me again. "Would you like to dance?"

"Um, I guess so." Why didn't I say no? I never danced in public unless I'd had a lot to drink, and even then, not to such weird music. I gulped a few mouthfuls of my drink, tasting the sweet, stinging alcohol, hoping it would help.

Sarah watched me follow the guy to the dance floor with a smirk on her face. I hoped she'd stay at the table until I got back, otherwise we'd lose our spot.

Out on the floor, the guy started moving to the music, and for a moment, I stood still and watched him. He motioned for me to join him. Self-consciously, I closed my eyes and let myself move to the beat of the music. Even without much alcohol, I could feel myself flowing with the sound, becoming part of the music. I felt his hand on my waist and his warm breath on my neck.

"You look beautiful, dancing like that. You should do it more often."

I opened my eyes and stopped dancing. "What's your name?"

He smiled. "David. What's yours?"

"Marielle."

"Nice to meet you, Marielle. Shall we keep dancing?"

"I think I need some more alcohol, actually." I went back to the table, and Sarah was nowhere to be seen. Oh well, at least my drink and belongings were still there. I sat down and finished my Archers. A minute later, David appeared at my side, holding out a glass.

"I guessed you must be drinking vodka?"

I shook my head, but took the drink anyway. Vodka wasn't my favourite, but any alcohol was fine with me. For some reason I just felt like getting a little tipsy, so that I could have some fun.

I drank the vodka and lemonade quite quickly, though it stung my throat. It was definitely a double.

I went back out onto the dance floor with David, and as I began to move, I could feel the alcohol beginning to take effect. The music seemed to be pulsing through me, and I could feel every note. David's hands were on my back and waist, pulling me in closer to his body as he moved to the music.

"What did you say?" I said in his ear, opening my eyes. He pulled back a little and shook his head.

"I didn't say anything."

"Oh." I closed my eyes again and carried on dancing. I could have sworn I'd heard a voice whisper something in my ear. Suddenly I was feeling a little dizzy, so I stopped moving to steady myself.

"Are you alright?"

I nodded to David, then gestured toward the toilets. He nodded and released me. I made my way to the ladies', but was feeling more unsteady on my feet by the second. I was a bit confused, as it normally took a lot more than two drinks to get me this drunk.

Luckily, there was no queue and I fumbled my way into one of the tiny cubicles. I sat on the toilet and had to close my eyes to stop everything from spinning. I suddenly realised I'd left my bag at the table, along with my coat.

"Shit." It may be a university event, but that didn't mean there was no crime. Stuff still got nicked. I breathed deeply, trying to clear my head, then somehow managed to stand up and get the door open. I ran my wrists under the cold tap for a while to try and cool myself off. I looked at my reflection in the mirror and a ridiculously pale version of me stared back.

I closed my eyes when my face started to blur and double. I felt like I could just curl up and go to sleep. I took a deep breath and opened my eyes again. I was just being silly. I couldn't possibly be that drunk. I would just get some water and everything would be fine.

The last thing I remembered was opening the door and heading into the darkened, throbbing room full of half-naked people.

Chapter Four

What would people do without a guardian angel watching over them? Not that I'm an angel, because I'm not. But since being in this dimension, I've seen the angels working tirelessly to keep people safe. Battling every day with people's stupid decisions. I see them trying to get through, but so often, their help is shunned by souls who just don't realise they are there. Who just don't listen to their intuition, their inner voice.

I wish she had listened to me tonight. I didn't know exactly what would happen, but when Sarah had suggested going out, I had the sense it would be a bad idea. After watching the guy with his hands all over her on the dance floor, the feeling got a lot stronger.

It isn't really my place to do so, after all, like I said, I'm not an angel, but I feel like I need to keep her safe. That it is important to do so. Her guardian angel is trying to help her too, but he isn't getting through, so he makes no move to stop me from stepping in.

When she leaves the toilets and re-enters the main room, she looks like she's going to pass out. Her pupils are heavily dilated, her skin is even paler than before. I hadn't been watching the guy closely, but I have the feeling he must have added something to the drink he gave her earlier.

If it were possible to feel anger here in this place, in this dimension, I'm pretty sure I would be really angry right now. I know that at this moment in time, he is waiting for her, just a few feet away, and I just can't let anything happen to her. So I summon all the energy available to me and I whisper in her ear. *Let's go get your coat and bag, and get you home.*

She nods, like she's heard me, and relief courses through my soul. It seems that being in this drugged state makes her more receptive to me, to hearing me.

I support her energetically as she moves through the room, and with her guardian angel's help, I make her appear invisible to the guy. She picks up her belongings (still safe because I made sure of it) and then she moves to the entrance. Her zombie-like appearance doesn't seem to be alarming anyone, but I realise that most of the people are too stoned or drunk to notice. I can't see Sarah, and can only assume she's gone somewhere with the guy who'd been chatting her up while Marielle had been dancing. I put in a silent request to her guardian angel to try and keep her safe.

Once Marielle is outside, I stay by her side, energetically willing her to keep walking, to stay focused. Her angel walks on her other side, helping me to keep her upright. Judging by the glazed look on her face, it seems like she isn't entirely aware of her surroundings or her actions. I keep whispering words of encouragement, and soon we are within sight of her building.

I tell her to get her key out, and she does, only fumbling a little to get it into the lock. Once inside, I guide her to the kitchen to get some water before going to her room and locking the door behind her. Within minutes, she is in bed, and the light is out. She becomes unconscious very quickly, and I begin to think that perhaps I should have got her to seek medical attention. What if she reacts badly to the drug that he's spiked her drink with?

I wonder if I should influence someone else to come and make sure she is okay. I move closer to her and listen to her breathing. It is even and steady, and though still pale, she doesn't seem to be too hot or too cold. I decide to just stay by her side, and at any sign of difficulty, I will raise the alarm. Her angel looks at me and nods, in agreement with my assessment and thoughts.

I like watching her sleep. I wish I could meet her in her dreams, but it hasn't worked so far. I feel quite strongly that when she finally realises I am here, when she finally acknowledges me, it will be the beginning of a bond that will never be broken.

*   *   *

At first I thought the hammering was inside my own skull. It took several minutes for me to realise it was coming from outside.

"Marielle?"

I opened one eye, and immediately closed it. It was far too bright. Much brighter than it normally was on an autumn morning.

The hammering started again. "Marielle?"

I knew it was Sarah. And from the panicked tinge to her voice, she was freaking out about something.

Thud, thud, thud. "Are you in there?"

Moving with extreme care, ever so slowly, I eased back the covers. Eyes still closed, I moved into a sitting position. It took all my strength to push myself up off the bed. What the hell happened last night?

More hammering and calling occurred before I could reach the door, my hands feeling the walls to guide me. I couldn't seem to speak to respond to her. I peered through slits at the lock. I was surprised I had managed to lock it properly the night before. I opened the door and nearly got hit by Sarah's fist.

"Oh, thank God!" She flung her arms around me, and the jolt nauseated me to the pit of my stomach. "I was so worried about you. What happened? Are you okay? It's two o'clock in the afternoon, I was beginning to think you were dead!"

She might not have been shouting, but I winced at the loudness of her voice in my ear and pulled away. "I'm fine," I mumbled quietly.

She looked at me more closely. "You look like shit, what happened? What did that guy do to you?"

"Guy? What guy?" I moved back into my room and got back into bed. Sarah followed me in, the heavy door thumping closed behind her.

"The guy you were dancing with?"

I rummaged around in my befuddled mind for a memory of the night before, but came up blank. I vaguely remembered talking to a guy right at the beginning of the evening, but I couldn't even really recall what he looked like.

"You don't remember? Christ, how much did you drink?"

Instead of responding, I laid down in bed and pulled the covers back up.

"I'll get you a cup of tea, I'm going to leave your door open so I can check on you later, okay?"

I nodded and heard Sarah's footsteps moving away. Within moments, I was asleep again.

Chapter Five

Time has no meaning to me anymore. I can see the hands on the clock moving, and I can see the sun crossing the sky, but I don't have the sense that any time is actually passing me by.

I don't think time exists here. Wherever here is. And I don't really know what to make of that. This endless, infinite, non-linear existence is strange. I exist, yet I have no body. I can observe and even at times influence those on earth, yet they are unaware of me. Time passes for them, but I remain the same. Having no body, and therefore no reflection, I have no idea of my appearance, or if I even have one. And that is a weird thing too. I don't need to breathe, and I feel no emotions, though I am aware of the emotions I would have felt if I were still human.

Everything seems brighter here. I can see all of the layers of existence, all overlapping one another, all mixed up together. There is the physical realm, the mental realm, the metaphysical realm and the spiritual realm. Each of these layers is made up of different colours. The physical and mental realms are quite grey in comparison to the spiritual realm and metaphysical realms. What incredible colours they contain. Most of which I have never seen before. I won't even attempt to describe them, to do so, I feel, would dim their magic.

I am simultaneously aware of several things at once,

even though they are in different geographical locations. I am aware of Sarah making tea in the kitchen, and I know she is very worried about her friend. Though apparently she hadn't worried at all last night when she found out Marielle had left. I am aware that the guy who drugged Marielle tried to do the same thing to another girl, and got beaten up by the girl's boyfriend, to the point where he ended up unconscious on the floor and was eventually taken away in an ambulance.

So karma works. It is a concept that eluded me when I was alive. It makes me wonder if my own death happened in order to strike some sort of karmic balance. Or perhaps it was just part of a larger design.

I think about what Marielle said the other day. About her having a crush on me when we were in school together. I wish I'd known. Because I liked her too. I never for a second thought she would ever look at me, ever feel that way about me, so of course I never did anything about my feelings.

I watch her sleeping, and I imagine touching her face, and seeing her eyes light up at the sight of me. Would it have worked? Us being together?

She sighs softly in her sleep, and I want to sigh too.

I guess we will never know.

*   *   *

Somehow, it was Sunday afternoon. Where had Saturday gone? I felt more alive and awake after taking a long shower, so I tried once more to remember what had happened, but drew a blank. I could vaguely remember a male voice close to my ear, but had no memory of what he'd said.

I got dressed and headed to the kitchen, suddenly

ravenous. I felt like I hadn't eaten in days. I paused as I opened the fridge. Huh. That was probably because I actually hadn't.

I pulled out the ingredients I needed for an omelette and soon filled the kitchen with the smell of onions.

"Hey, stranger, how are you feeling now?"

I looked up and smiled at Sarah. "Much better. What the hell happened?"

Sarah shook her head, and I could see the worry in her eyes. "I don't know. You went and danced with that cute guy, then I got chatting to someone and went to sit at their table. When I came back to tell you I was heading off, your coat and bag were gone, you were nowhere to be seen, and when I asked, a few people said you'd left with some guy."

I frowned. "I did? I really don't remember. They actually saw me leaving with someone?"

"Yep." Sarah stole one of my tomatoes and popped it into her mouth.

"The same guy I was dancing with?"

Sarah shrugged. "I guess so, I didn't see him after that."

"Where did you go?"

Sarah looked down and blushed.

"Come on, spill. I want details," I said, adding the tomatoes to the frying pan.

"You know that guy I told you about? From my theology class?"

I nodded. I had a vague memory of her mentioning someone a week ago.

"It was him. We started chatting and well, went back to his dorm room." She held her hands up. "Nothing happened. Okay, we did kiss, but that was it. Then he walked me back here. Your light was off, and you weren't answering your phone, so I figured you must have either gone back with that guy or you were asleep."

"Hmm, maybe in the future we should have some sort of system. Anything could have happened to either of us. I was completely wasted, somehow. I have no idea what happened to the guy I left with."

"You're right. I'm sorry I didn't look after you better." She leaned her head on my shoulder and I smiled.

"It's okay. We both lived to tell the tale. I might just stay away from fetish nights in the future though."

Sarah laughed. "Fair enough."

I gestured to the pan on the stove. "Want some omelette?"

"Sure, sounds good. I've been so busy writing my essay that I haven't been out to buy any food."

"Ugh, I've got so much work to do, and I seem to have slept away the entire weekend."

"It was a pretty extreme hangover. Are you sure your drink wasn't spiked or something?"

I shrugged. "No idea." I finished making the omelette and served it up with salad. I set the plate in front of Sarah and sat across the table from her.

"So are you going to see him again?"

Sarah's forkful of salad paused just before it entered her mouth. "Yeah, we're meeting for a drink tonight actually."

"That's great. What's he like?"

Sarah launched into a detailed description of her new guy, and I pushed away the thoughts swirling around my mind of the mystery man who had taken me home on Friday. I wondered if I would ever find out who he was.

*　　　*　　　*

For someone who has no sense of time, Monday morning cannot come soon enough for me. I know Jane has written the letter I influenced her to write. And it should be arriving this morning.

But Marielle doesn't go to the main building until the end of the day, after all of her classes. I had no real interest in politics when I was alive, and I have even less interest now. During her classes I feel impatient, though I know it is just imagined. I know that as soon as she gets Jane's letter, she will finally realise that I'm here with her.

Won't she?

I'm with her as she walks to the main building and heads for the mail cubbyholes. Considering it is the age of e-mail, she still always gets a considerable number of hand-written letters. I like that. It shows people care enough about her to put pen to paper and post it.

She sorts through the mail, then begins opening the letters as she walks back to her dorm building. She opens all the boring stuff first: the eye-test reminder, the bank statement and the mobile phone bill. She reaches her building and once inside, goes straight to the kitchen. She makes herself a cup of tea and sits at the kitchen table. She opens a notecard from her gran and a letter from a friend in America, before finally opening Jane's letter. I read it over her shoulder. Ninety-nine percent of it is just ordinary, everyday stuff. Finally, there it is. In the postscript at the very bottom.

P.S. Do you remember Nathan, from school? He passed away a few weeks ago.

I know when she reaches that sentence. That lone, simple sentence. Because her hand starts shaking, and she nearly drops her mug.

I want to see her face, but am suddenly unsure as to what I will see. Will she be upset? Indifferent? Will my death bother her at all?

The single tear that hits the table speaks volumes.

She puts the letter down and picks up her mug, cradling it in both hands.

"Hey, Marielle. How's it going?"

Marielle jumps and looks up at one of her dorm mates, Susie. She nods and quickly wipes her eyes while Susie is looking in the fridge.

"Yeah, I'm good, you?" Her voice is unsteady, but only I notice.

"Alright, just got a ridiculous amount of research to do." Susie closes the fridge, now armed with a large bottle of diet coke. "See you later."

She leaves the room before Marielle can reply.

Marielle seems to be moving in slow motion. She finishes her tea, washes and dries her mug, gathers her letters and heads for her room. I feel maybe I should leave her alone for a while. It feels like I am intruding. But at the same time, I need to see if she makes the connection now. If she finally figures out I am with her. And that I want to help her.

Back in her room, she sits on her bed and stares into space.

When I was alive, I hadn't experienced many people dying. I hadn't gone through the stages of grief. So I'm not entirely sure what to expect. I know everyone grieves in their own way, and I have no way of knowing how Marielle will react.

I watch her for a while, but she doesn't move, she doesn't cry, she doesn't really do anything at all. She just sits there, frozen.

I wish I could know what she is thinking.

Chapter Six

Nathan is dead.

Inside the frozen exterior, my mind felt jagged and chaotic as it tried to work out what it all meant. All of the signs and messages I'd been getting that referred to Nathan, had been in the last couple of weeks, since he'd died. How had he died? He was only twenty-one, like me. People our age shouldn't be dying. It wasn't right. Had he done all he wanted to do with his life? Had he fallen in love, had his heart broken, laughed enough?

I felt completely devastated, which seemed strange as we had barely known each other. I didn't think he'd known about my crush on him, and therefore must have had no idea I'd thought he was really cute.

He's dead.

Every time the thought crashed through my mind, my heart shuddered and thudded and stalled. Was it weird to feel so bereft?

I had no idea how long I sat there, but when the knocking on the door finally pierced my consciousness, and I moved to open it, I felt stiff, my muscles were locked into position.

"Hey, I was just wondering..." Sarah peered at me closely and frowned. "What's wrong?"

I shrugged, and a second tear escaped. I didn't even attempt to speak.

Sarah guided me back into my room and sat me down on the bed. "Has something happened again? You're as white as a ghost."

I blinked. Ghost. It had been my favourite movie in the nineties. Patrick Swayze, Demi Moore, the pottery wheel.

Was Nathan haunting me?

"Hello?" Fingers clicked in front of my face. "Are you there?"

I looked at Sarah. "I'm sorry, it's nothing. I'm fine, honestly. Just feeling a bit fluey."

The frown on her face suggested she wasn't convinced. She leaned over and touched my forehead, making me feel about five years old.

"You don't have a temperature. Would you like some honey and lemon?"

I nodded, managing to hold back further tears. Being treated with sympathy when I was dangerously close to breaking down was never a good thing.

Sarah left the room and I tried to pull myself together. I couldn't explain why I felt the need to keep it to myself, but telling Sarah about Nathan's death didn't feel right. It felt like it was something I needed to deal with on my own.

I looked around my room, and suddenly felt like someone was watching me. At that exact second, the light began to flicker.

When Sarah came back, minutes later, the light returned to normal.

"Here, drink this. And take one of these," she held out a bottle of vitamin C. I dutifully did as I was told, and Sarah patted me on the shoulder, then left, saying to call her if I needed anything.

Alone again, I read Jane's letter a second time, and wondered if she knew any more information about Nathan. Though we were all in the same year, I hadn't realised she'd even really been aware of Nathan, as she didn't share any of his classes. Should I call her?

My hand hovered over my mobile phone, uncertain. Just then, my TV switched itself on. I jumped at the noise of a chocolate advert blaring out from the tiny screen. I found the remote on my bedside table and switched it off. What was going on with the electrics today?

I sat in silence for a while. Finally, figuring I had nothing to lose, I picked up my phone and rang Jane.

*   *   *

Why is it taking so long? She asked for a sign, and Jane's letter is so clear. Why won't she acknowledge that I'm here?

"Nathan."

I look up, thinking that she realises I am here, only to find Marielle's guardian angel addressing me.

"Yes?" I ask.

"Why is your need to connect with her so great?"

Good question. I have asked myself that many times, since passing on and finding myself drawn to her.

"The reason is still unclear to me, but I know it's important."

Her angel seems to be considering my words. "I think you may be right. I will help in any way I can, but you know I cannot tamper with her free will."

"I know. Thank you."

I hadn't expected to get any help with my mission, but it is nice to know it is available if I need it. When I was alive, I rarely allowed anyone to help me. Too stubborn to admit I needed any at times. It's weird, how it seems to be so important to be self-sufficient and independent. Yet when you cross over, you realise how you are connected to everyone and everything, and any attempts to become separate are likely to lead to your demise rather than your destiny.

Marielle finishes speaking to Jane, having found out a few more details of my death. Though the details she's been given aren't entirely accurate. What the papers had reported hadn't been the full story, but it hardly matters now.

She looks at the clock on her desk and suddenly jumps up. After moving with glacial slowness since reading the letter, she is now moving with a speed and efficiency I've never seen in her before. She puts her coat on and grabs her bag and is out of the door in seconds. I follow her, intrigued by her sudden decision to do something.

Ten minutes later, she enters the Black Swan Bookshop and heads straight to the mediumship section.

"Hello, can I help you at all?"

Marielle looks up at the shop owner, and shrugs. "I'm looking for something on communication with spirits. Any recommendations?"

"Certainly." The lady joins Marielle and pulls out a few titles. She hands them to her and Marielle flicks through them. She stops at a particular page in one, and nods.

"I'll take this one." She puts the rest back and follows the lady to the counter.

"Everything alright?"

It is an innocent question, but I can sense the concern behind it.

Marielle shrugs again. "Yeah, I've just been meaning to do some reading on this for a while, and I just thought I'd pop by and see if you had anything."

Blatant lies. Interesting. Why does Marielle feel the need to keep this a secret? To keep me a secret? Is she worried about what people might think?

"I hope it's useful. If you have any questions, I have a friend who's a medium, who I'm sure would be more than happy to answer them."

Marielle nods and receives the book in exchange for her money. She leaves and the lady turns the sign on the door behind her and locks it. I now understand her sudden urgency to get there.

She goes straight back to her room, and lays on her bed with her new book.

Getting the feeling she won't be moving for a while, I leave her to it.

Chapter Seven

By the time Sarah knocked on my door later that evening, I had learned more about mediumship than I had ever thought possible.

"How are you feeling?"

I frowned, having forgotten I'd said I had the flu. "Fine, just felt a bit weird earlier."

"Have you had dinner?"

I looked at the clock, it was nearly nine. "No, I forgot."

Sarah shook her head. "Come on, I made potato and leek soup and there's far too much for just me."

"No, thank you, I'll have something later."

She dragged me out of my room, down the hall to the kitchen, not taking no for an answer.

I don't even remember the taste of the soup, or the bread, or whether we even spoke. My mind was on Nathan.

Was he really here? Was he really trying to talk to me? The flickering lights, the voice, the feeling of being watched... In my new book they were all signs there was a spirit present. But so far, the book hadn't mentioned a clear cut way to communicate with the spirit. Maybe I should go and ask the lady in the Black Swan for the contact details of the medium she mentioned.

"Huh?" I looked up at Sarah and felt a twinge of guilt that she had to try so hard to get my attention.

Sarah was shaking her head. "Are you sure you're okay? You're really starting to worry me."

I tried to smile. "I'm fine, really. I've just got so much on my mind, I'm finding it hard to stay present and not get lost in my thoughts."

Sarah frowned. "You know you can talk to me about anything, don't you?"

I nodded, and this time managed a more genuine smile. "I know, and sometime soon I will take you up on that, I promise. I just feel like I need to deal with these things by myself for now."

Sarah was quiet for a while, and I wondered if she really believed me. She cleared away our bowls and started washing up.

After a few moments, I joined her at the sink. I picked up a tea towel and started to dry the dishes. Though intending to stay in the present, within seconds I was back in my own world again, wondering what I should do about Nathan.

*   *   *

I'm so close now. I can feel it. Any moment now she will truly realise I am here. That the energy surrounding her is me. She will speak my name, and I will no longer exist in this half-state. I will be with her. I don't know how, and I don't know what it will feel like. I don't even know if it will be any different, but I know we will be closer, somehow.

Watching her read the book on mediumship is fascinating. She's a fast reader, so shortly after dinner she's nearly finished it. Every now and then she looks up and her gaze seems to rest on the area where I exist. I read a few words over her shoulder, feeling amused when I read the list of all the ways a spirit makes itself known. The only part I don't agree with, is when it mentions that good spirits make you feel warm and tingly, and bad spirits make you feel cold.

Because I've noticed that when I am near her, her skin breaks out in goose bumps, and her hairs stand on end. When awake, she rubs her arms, unconscious of the fact that I am causing it, perhaps assuming she is merely cold. When asleep, she shivers whenever I am near.

I am not a bad spirit. And neither have I seen any, from where I exist. Wherever this is. Perhaps there are such things as 'bad' spirits. But I know they do not exist on this plane. All I have seen are angels. I haven't even seen another soul like myself. Perhaps we are invisible to each other. Or perhaps I am the only one.

When she reads the last page, and sets the book on the bedside table, I wait. Will she try to contact me? If only she would realise that all she needs to do is speak my name. It is so simple. Humans do not need books to tell them how to speak to us. There are no methods. No right ways or wrong ways. We are here. We are listening. Well, I am listening.

"So am I." I look up and see Marielle's angel, and acknowledge him. Yes, the angels are listening too.

So why won't Marielle listen to me? I see that she seems to be in a meditative state, and decide to try once more. I concentrate and make the TV switch on. This time, she doesn't jump, but just stares at it. Before she can get to the remote control, I turn it off. I switch her DVD player on, and off again. Then her computer. Finally, I make the lights flicker. I can sense what can only be described as slight disapproval emanating from her angel, as angels never judge, but I can sense he thinks I am going overboard.

I stop disrupting the electrics and watch Marielle's face

closely. Finally, after what seems like an eternity of silence, I hear her beautiful voice whisper.

"Nathan?"

*   *   *

I tossed and turned that night. It was difficult to fall asleep when I knew there was someone watching me. Just the thought made me shiver. Was it true only bad spirits made you feel cold? I had been freezing cold the whole time the strange occurrences had been going on. Was Nathan a bad spirit? Or was it a bad spirit pretending to be Nathan? What did the spirit want, anyway? Surely if they were trying to get a message to someone, they'd go through a proper medium?

I sighed and stared at the darkened ceiling. The orange light of the streetlamps outside gave the room an eerie glow.

Despite reading an entire book on the matter, I was still not quite sure how to talk to the spirit. Should I ask him to make the lights flicker once for yes, twice for no?

It seemed crazy, lying awake in bed wondering how to contact a dead person. I squeezed my eyes shut and willed myself to fall asleep, but just couldn't switch off my thoughts. Finally, I gave up and reached over to flick the lamp on, pulling out my notebook from the drawer. Maybe I could write some poetry or something to...

I froze suddenly, my hand still on my notebook. Writing. The weird things I'd been writing in the last week or so. I flipped open the cover and skipped straight to the stream of consciousness I wrote in creative writing class. I read it silently, and without warning, tears began to stream down my face.

It was Nathan. I was sure of it. And by speaking his

name, I had called him to me. Did that mean he was no longer in between? Did that mean he was now with me? I picked up the pen from my bedside table, and flipped to a new page. Hand shaking slightly, I put the nib to the page and waited.

I didn't have to wait long.

*   *   *

How amazing it is! It is as though my spirit has blended with hers and as one our thoughts mingle and blend and spill through the pen onto the page.

She cannot deny I am here now. She cannot resist it. And together we will work out why this unusual alliance has been made. Together we will work out the connection between our souls.

With our strengthened bond, I find I can sense Marielle's emotions now. It is an odd feeling, considering I have not felt any emotions since leaving the physical realm. Even then, I was not an overly emotional person. I suppose to most I seemed to be a typical guy. It's funny to think that nothing I ever worried about while I was alive matters in the slightest now.

I can sense Marielle is tiring, and though her hand is moving of its own accord (with my help), her eyelids are drooping. I send her the thought that she should stop, switch the light off and sleep, and without hesitation, she does exactly that. Within minutes, she is sleeping soundly. I think of the words I have given her and I feel a peaceful sense of happiness and anticipation. I don't know if it is my own feeling, or hers. But I know that tomorrow the world will look completely different to her. Tomorrow will be the beginning of our adventure.

Chapter Eight

I didn't wake up slowly the next morning, I went from being soundly asleep to wide awake. My eyes opened suddenly, but for once, the dim morning light didn't bother me.

I felt strange. Like I wasn't properly in my body. I could vaguely recall dreams of flying and wondered if I had been travelling astrally while my body slept. I'd have to re-read that section of the mediumship book later. I sat up and my eyes rested on my notebook. Suddenly, I recalled my late night scribbling, but I couldn't remember what I'd written.

I flipped the notebook open. My usually very messy scrawl seemed incredibly neat on the page.

Once a bond like this is formed, it can never be broken. Though we may not have known each other well in the physical world, we are now as one. I feel everything you feel. You need to learn to trust in your intuition and inner feelings, because they are my way of guiding you. Though I may not know all that is happening in your future, I do get feelings about what may be good for you, and so will pass that information to you through our bond. So please listen. I wish nothing more for you than pure love, joy and happiness. Your smile, your laughter, it brightens not only my existence but all of those who come into contact with you. You are so beautiful, the light of your soul shines in all directions, throughout all of the layers, through all of time. If you ever feel afraid or upset, I'm here. Just whisper my name, and I will answer. Your guardian angel is here too. Between us, we will keep you safe, always.

I couldn't stop the tears from falling again. Such sweet words. I could feel he truly cared for me, and that he was watching over me. The feeling of being watched was now more comforting than creepy, and I knew that with him by my side, everything was going to be just fine.

A knock at the door made me jump and drop the notebook. I reached down, picked it up and after putting it on my desk, crossed the tiny room to the door. I opened it to find Sarah standing there. She looked me up and down and frowned.

"Are you still ill? We have English Lit in ten minutes."

I shook my head. "No, I'm fine, more than fine, I just overslept a little. I'll get ready and I'll see you there. No sense in both of us being late."

Sarah nodded, but still looked concerned. "Try not to be too long, you know what a battle-axe old Cynthia can be."

I smiled. I certainly did know. I was already on the English Lit Professor's shit list for being late too many times this term. "I'll be as quick as I can."

Dashing back into my room, I quickly brushed my teeth, got changed into jeans and a jumper and ran a brush through my hair. I couldn't be bothered with make-up, perhaps if I looked really pale, Cynthia wouldn't give me too hard a time for being late. I grabbed my bag and some extra pens and ran out of the door.

As soon as the icy blast of air hit my face I shivered and wished I'd grabbed my coat. At least the English building was just a few metres away. I sprinted across the dewy grass. Luckily it was a large class and I was able to slip into the back row without causing too much of a commotion.

Cynthia acknowledged my entrance with a raised eyebrow, but made no comment, and continued the introduction to her lecture. I looked down at the desk and smiled. Normally the disapproval of a professor would bother me, but today I realised it really didn't matter.

Not for the first time, I noticed that if I let my gaze relax a little as I stared at the white board, I could see different coloured outlines around all the people sat in front of me, as well as around the professor. I had seen these colours before, but I'd never wondered what it was.

I looked down at my notebook and found the answer.

They are auras. The different colours signify different emotions.

I smiled again. Nathan was here. But that made sense, considering the bond we now shared. I looked up again at my classmates and tried to distinguish the different colours I could see around them.

Red is passion. But could also be anger or frustration.

Orange is creativity. If it's a really deep, dark orange, it's unexpressed creativity.

Yellow is happiness. Excitement.

Blue is calm. Serenity. A knowing that all is well.

Green is healing. If it's a dark green, healing is needed. If it's a light green, a healing energy is radiating from them.

Purple is spirituality. Those with purple auras are usually attuned to a higher consciousness, if not all the time, at least some of the time. They are aware of the web of energy connecting us all.

White or gold is an angelic colour. Those with white or gold auras were angels in past lives, and they now roam the earth as humans, helping those in need.

I read through what I had just written, fascinated again by the way Nathan was communicating with me.

The section in the mediumship book on automatic writing hadn't really gone into detail about how it worked, but I could only assume this is what it meant.

I looked up and was surprised to notice that the colour around Cynthia was blue. Considering her attitude, I would have assumed it would have been red. Perhaps there was an underlying serenity beneath her irritated exterior.

The class was over before I had actually taken in anything Cynthia had said. I looked down at my notes and all I'd written were Nathan's words. If I didn't start paying attention soon, I was going to fail my classes.

I packed away my things and Sarah came and found me at the back of the room.

"Hey, don't you think that was interesting? What she said about Emily Brontë?"

I zipped up my bag and looked around to make sure Cynthia wasn't within earshot. "Um, actually I wasn't listening to the lecture at all, I was distracted."

"Distracted? By what?"

"I'll tell you later, I better get to my next class." I followed Sarah out of the building, and after a concerned and confused look in my direction, Sarah headed back to the dorm.

After paying absolutely no attention whatsoever to my history lecturer for the next couple of hours, I headed back to the dorm, knowing that sometime soon I was going to have some major catching up to do.

I went to the kitchen and found Sarah sat at the table, reading a book. She glanced up when I entered, and I put the kettle on, to make us both a cup of tea. I set the steaming mug in front of her, and had barely sat down when Sarah prompted me to talk.

"It's hard to explain."

"Well, I know something's up, you've been really strange the last couple of weeks."

I laughed. "I'm always strange."

"Okay, you've been stranger than usual then."

"Yeah, I guess I have." I sighed. I still felt reluctant to share what had been happening, but it would be nice to be able to talk about it with someone. I trusted Sarah implicitly, and she was pretty open minded. I was sure she wouldn't get me carted off to the nearest mental hospital.

"I'm just going to say what's been happening, you don't have to believe me, but I swear it's all true."

*   *   *

It's interesting to hear Marielle describe what has been happening in the last couple of weeks. I don't think she'd actually put all the events together until she started telling Sarah about it. I can see from her face that everything is now clicking into place.

Sarah seems to be taking it all in without judgement, just nodding her head and listening. I can't tell from her face what she thinks of it all, because I don't know her very well. I look up at Sarah's guardian angel, and she nods at me. I haven't asked them outright, but I believe the angels can hear their thoughts. In which case, whatever is going through Sarah's mind must be positive. Which is good. I don't know why Marielle felt compelled to keep it a secret until now. I think it will be good for her to have someone to share it with.

Marielle finishes her explanation and is waiting for Sarah's response.

"Wow. I must admit, I'd never have guessed that was what was going on."

"Do you believe me?"

Sarah nods slowly. "Yes. I know you. If you think this ghost, this spirit, is really here, and is communicating with you, then I believe it is."

Marielle looks relieved. "Problem is, I just can't concentrate on anything. I'm missing everything in my classes because whenever I relax, and start writing,

Nathan's words come through, not notes on the lecture."

"Maybe you can ask him not to come through when you're in class?"

I feel bad. Or rather, if I were human right now, I would feel bad. I don't want to mess up Marielle's studies, that is not my intention. But I'm not entirely sure what my intention is. Now she knows I am with her, now I can communicate easily with her, what's supposed to happen now? What's the purpose of our bond? I still have no idea.

"Yes you do."

I look around, but neither Marielle, Sarah nor their angels have spoken. "No I don't," I respond.

"You know exactly why you are connected. You just need to remember."

I don't know who is talking to me. I can't sense or see anyone. But apparently I know why this is all happening. Interesting.

I'm not really listening to their conversation now. Immersed in my own thoughts, I suddenly notice I am alone in the kitchen. I move back to Marielle's side, and find her in her room, pen in hand, notebook in front of her on the desk. By her closed eyes, I assume she is waiting for me.

Without another second's hesitation, I start talking to her.

I'm here.

Her eyes open and she looks down at the words on the page.

"Tell me why," she whispers.

I have been afraid of this question. Because I'm still not sure why, despite what the voice said earlier.

I am here for you. To protect you. The words flow through her pen before they are really formed in my consciousness, so maybe I do know why.

I also came here for a second chance with you.

Marielle's eyes widen and I also feel what would have been surprise. A second chance? How is that even possible? Where are these words coming from? They're not coming from me. And I can't sense anyone else nearby.

Her pen touches the paper, and the words start flowing again. This time, I get a sense of where they are coming from. They seem to be coming from above where I exist.

Do you want to be with me?

Marielle is still for a while, and I suddenly know what the words mean. And I know what would happen if she said-

"Yes."

Chapter Nine

"Marielle?"

Her head whipped round and she looked right at me. "Nathan?" she whispered back, standing up from her chair and taking a step toward me. "Is that really you?"

Considering a dead person had suddenly shown up in the flesh, so to speak, in her bedroom, she was surprisingly calm. I nodded. It seemed like a long time since I had spoken properly, since I had been seen and heard by a human.

She took another step toward me, her hand stretched out slightly. She touched my arm and a shiver ran through her. "How can I see you? How can I feel you?"

I looked down at my arm, where her fingertips were warming my skin, and the sight of my own body was slightly jarring after my formless existence. The touch of her fingertips was also jarring, but in a much more pleasant way. I had forgotten what physical contact felt like. I looked into her eyes, which were a light grey colour, not something I had noticed before, and I struggled to find words to explain.

"Am I dead too?" she asked, her fingers gripping my arm suddenly, a look of fear flitting across her face.

I shook my head. I didn't think she was dead. But I didn't think I had suddenly come back to life, either. I looked around, but all I could see was her room. Her angel was invisible to me, and I realised the thoughts in my head were purely my own, I could hear no other ethereal beings.

"Nathan?" She had moved a little closer while my thoughts were whirring, and I could smell the scent of her perfume. It was sweet, but subtle. Much like her. I was still finding it difficult to form words, so I decided to do what I had wanted to since the first night I had watched her sleep. I stroked the side of her face, and once again she shivered. But she didn't move away, or stop me. I tilted her face up, and I leaned down slowly, wanting her to stop me if she felt uncomfortable, but she didn't. When my lips finally met hers, my thoughts fell silent, and I knew I was where I belonged.

*   *   *

The moment my lips touched his, my mind was thrown into chaos. I was kissing Nathan. Nathan. The guy I'd gone to school with. It was definitely him. Ridiculously tall, dark brown hair, dark brown eyes.

But he's dead, the logical part of my brain screamed at me. *He's dead. How can he be here, in my room, kissing me?*

At the same time I quietly told the logical voice to hush, because I knew something magical was happening. What we were doing shouldn't have been possible, but somehow it felt more right than anything else had in my whole life.

I melted into his arms and he lifted me up. Goodness, I had forgotten how tall he was. I wrapped my legs around his waist and we continued to kiss, melded into one another.

His strength, his passion, his scent, which I didn't remember from when I knew him before, all felt familiar to me. My senses were overwhelmed, yet I felt calm. Like I had finally come home.

After a few minutes, I pulled back a little and looked into his eyes. Though I didn't really want to break the intensity of the moment with talking, I needed to know, I needed to work out what was going on. "I don't understand. How is this happening?"

Nathan sighed and still holding me tight, he turned and sat on the edge of my bed. After several moments, when he finally spoke, the sound of his voice made me shiver again.

"I'm not entirely sure I understand it either," he said, and I could hear the truth in his words. "I think something happened when you said you wanted to be with me. Either you have crossed into my dimension, or I have crossed into yours, or somehow we have blended the two together."

I blinked. "Is that even possible? I mean, I've only really got into the mediumship thing recently, since you started trying to talk to me. But nothing I've read so far has suggested that this is possible." I frowned and stroked his cheek. "I mean, I can feel you. You're here, breathing and warm and real." I shook my head. "Even the mediums who can see spirits just see them as flat images or colours or impressions."

Nathan shook his head too. "I didn't know this was possible either, but I do know that where I was, anything was possible. So though being here with you now is surprising, at the same time it seems completely normal to me. Does that make sense?"

I smiled. "Not really." He began to speak again, but I put my finger to his lips. "Perhaps we can try to figure it out later. Right now, I think I'd rather be kissing you."

He smiled too, and the dimples in his cheeks reminded me of the smile he gave me in the memory I'd had under hypnosis. I leaned forward to kiss him, but just before our lips met, a loud knock on the door made me jump. If

Nathan hadn't been holding me so tightly I would have fallen backwards out of his arms.

"Marielle?"

I heard Sarah's muffled voice and sighed. I kissed Nathan quickly, then pulled away from him. "I'll get rid of her, don't go anywhere." He didn't reply, but just watched me as I went to answer the door.

"Hey," I said, trying to sound normal, and not just like I had been making out with a ghost. "What's up?"

Sarah frowned, not even remotely fooled by my cool act. "Is everything okay? I thought I heard you talking to someone." She tried to peer past me but I pulled the door close to me, blocking her view.

"Was just watching some videos on the internet," I replied, kicking myself for not having my TV or computer on. I would remember to play music next time. I'd forgotten how paper-thin the walls were between our rooms.

Sarah was still frowning, and I felt impatient to get back to Nathan. I couldn't hear him in the room behind me, but I didn't want to look to make sure he was there. "Shall we have dinner together later? I can make my famous lasagne?"

Finally, her frown smoothed out a little and Sarah nodded. "Okay, I'll see you in a bit."

I smiled, and stepped backwards to push the door closed. I turned back and had only taken a step into my room when I realised Nathan was no longer there.

"Nathan?" I called softly, thinking that perhaps he had just left momentarily to avoid being seen by Sarah. There was no reply. I crossed the room to my desk and grabbed a pen and some scrap paper. I held the nib a millimetre above the page for about fifteen minutes before I accepted he really wasn't there. I set the pen down and decided to go and start making dinner. I wondered whether he'd really been there at all. Had I imagined the whole thing?

Feeling a bit silly, I whispered into the empty room. "I'll be back later. Maybe I'll see you then?"

Shaking my head and wondering if I had gone completely insane, I headed for the kitchen.

*   *   *

I watch her leave and wonder what she is thinking. I can sense through our connection that she is feeling a whole range of emotions, from confusion to attraction.

I'm not entirely sure what happened. One minute I'm sat on her bed, watching her walk to the door, and the next, I'm back in my ethereal state, moving at the speed of thought again.

"You're back."

I look up and see Marielle's guardian angel looking at me, a smile on his face.

"I guess I am," I reply. "What happened? Will I be able to do that again, or was it a one-off?"

The angel shrugs. "I'm not entirely sure. We angels can do what you just did, become human, a living breathing soul, on the human plane, when we are meant to help those in dire situations. But I have not seen a spirit do it as you just did. I don't know if you will be able to do it again."

"I didn't realise you could become human," I said. I have not asked the angels many questions since I died, and I realise now that my knowledge of them is limited. "Have you done it?"

The angel smiles. "Yes. Why don't we continue this conversation in the kitchen? You know I need to keep a close watch on Marielle there. Between herself and her dorm mates, they have managed to set it on fire four times already this term."

I laugh and follow the angel to the kitchen, where Marielle is chopping up vegetables for her supposedly famous lasagne.

When we arrive in the kitchen, rock music is blasting out of the radio and Marielle is dancing a little while cooking. I smile at the way she moves, remembering the feel of her skin against mine, how it felt to hold her tightly around the waist. I wish I could dance with her now.

I move my focus from Marielle back to her guardian angel, who is waiting patiently for me. "What happened? When you became human?"

"It was during winter, a few years ago. Marielle was driving along the lanes,"

"You became human to save Marielle?" I cut in suddenly. I'm not sure why I am surprised, after all, he is Marielle's guardian angel.

"Yes. She is quite skilled at driving in the snow, but on this particular night she was in a hurry to get to the cinema on time to meet her friends, and she wasn't concentrating as much as she should have been. I could see that further up the road there was a lorry that was also going a little too fast for the conditions, and I calculated they would meet on a corner, and at those speeds, Marielle wouldn't stand a chance."

With his words, I know if I were in a human body, I would have gasped. The idea of Marielle's car colliding with a lorry on an icy road is just too horrible for my ethereal form to contemplate.

"So I became a human, and I pretended to be a hitchhiker. I knew she wouldn't be able to resist stopping to give me a lift, because it was freezing cold. She stopped to pick me up, and when I got in the car, I commented on how icy the road was, and how she should be careful on the next few bends. We encountered the lorry on a longer stretch where there were passing places. She was driving slowly enough that she was able to pull over and let the lorry pass."

"What happened then?" I ask, slightly concerned that Marielle picks up hitchhikers, after all, what if they aren't all angels?

"She dropped me off in the next town, and continued on to the cinema, where she was on time to meet her friends."

I watch Marielle dancing around the kitchen, pretending to sing into a wooden spoon for a few moments, when something occurs to me. I turn back to her angel. "Why didn't you just talk to her? Plant the suggestion in her mind she should slow down?"

"In some situations that is all that is needed, but if there is loud music playing, or if they are stressed, agitated, anxious or in a hurry, it is difficult to get through. Which is why we resort to becoming human."

"Have you saved her life many times?"

"A few." The guardian angel looks like he wants to say something else, but he remains silent.

"So where was my guardian angel?" I ask.

"He was with you the whole time. He had tried, earlier in the day, to warn you what was going to happen, but much like Marielle ignored your warning the other night, you chose to ignore it."

"Why didn't he try harder? Why didn't he turn into a human and save me?"

Marielle's guardian angel is quiet for a moment. "Because you had already chosen, before entering this lifetime, to leave at that age. It was meant to happen that way."

"Oh." I watch Marielle layering the vegetables, pasta

sheets and sauce in the glass dish before putting it in the hot oven. She starts cleaning up the mess she's made. I don't know what to say to the angel. What is there to say? It seems as though my death was of my own choosing. "Shouldn't I be able to remember making that decision? I mean, in between lives don't we get to remember everything that happened before? All I can remember at the moment is being in my last lifetime."

"You are not fully on the other side. You are in the angel dimension. If you were fully on the other side, yes you would remember everything. But you are not."

"So I'm stuck here, in between earth and the other side?"

"You are not stuck, you can choose to move on at any point. But saying that, it does appear that your life and Marielle's are intertwined, and for this moment, you are exactly where you should be."

*   *   *

Though I was already missing Nathan, I felt really very happy while making dinner. It had been ages since I'd put on some loud music and danced around, not worrying about anyone walking in and thinking I had completely lost it. Once the lasagne was ready, I plastered some bread with garlic butter and grilled it, knowing it was Sarah's favourite food, and the smell would bring her out of her room.

Sure enough, a couple of minutes later, she came into the kitchen.

"Mmmmm, smells amazing." She came over and gave me a sideways hug. "Thanks for making dinner. This essay is just killing me at the moment. I couldn't even think about cooking."

"You'd probably have more time to write if you weren't

so busy with Matt all the time." I stepped away to avoid her playful swipe and laughed.

"Oh, hush. You might be in your room studying all the time, but some of us like to have a life too."

It was my turn to blush. I couldn't actually remember when I last did some proper studying. In all the craziness of the last few days, my uni work had been the last thing on my mind. I vowed to get some research done later after eating.

"Sit down, I'll serve up," I said, getting plates out of the cupboard. I served the lasagne, then removed the garlic bread from the grill just moments before it would have started to burn.

We sat at the table and were quiet for a while, the only sounds the clinking of our cutlery on the china and the crunching of garlic bread.

"What's happened?" Sarah asked suddenly.

I looked up from my plate. "What do you mean?" For some reason, my heart started hammering.

"You look different. And you were weird earlier when I knocked on your door. So something must have happened."

I shook my head. "No, nothing in particular." I put another forkful of lasagne in my mouth.

"Is it something to do with Nathan? Have you had any more communication?"

I sucked in the mouthful in surprise and started choking on it. Sarah immediately jumped up and started thumping me on the back. After a moment I started coughing and managed to clear my air pipe. My cheeks were on fire and my throat was raw as I sipped some water to try and calm down. Sarah sat in her chair again, looking even more worried.

"That's it, isn't it, he's been in touch again, hasn't he?"

I knew I couldn't keep it a secret from her, we knew each other too well. She could read me too easily to be fooled by my lies.

"Yes." My voice was scratchy and I cleared my throat, wincing at the soreness.

"What did he say? Did you do the automatic writing again?"

I was torn between telling her some of the truth or all of it. I hadn't even fully processed the events from earlier in the day myself. And the more I thought about it, the more dream-like it became. How could I tell her about it and not sound insane? "Yes, it seems to be easier now, for him to talk through me. I ask questions and then I write his answers."

"That's so amazing. So what has he got to say? Have you asked him what it's like there? What it's like to be a ghost?"

I shook my head. "No, I hadn't really thought to. Mostly we've just talked about..." I stopped talking when I realised I was about to say 'how we should be together'. Because that just sounded crazy too.

Sarah paused her eating and was watching me, waiting for the end of my sentence. "About?" she prompted.

"About silly things. You're right, I should ask him what it's like and what he's been up to."

Sarah didn't look convinced that I'd given her the truthful ending to the sentence, but she didn't push it. "When you ask him those things, let me know, I'd love to know what it's like."

"I didn't realise you were so interested in the afterlife," I commented, glad the subject had shifted slightly.

Sarah shrugged. "It's comforting to know there is something else after you die. I grew up in a family of atheists. Once you were dead, you turned to ash or you decomposed in the ground, and that was that, you ceased to exist." Sarah shuddered. "I think that's why I turned to studying theology. Because I wanted to find out the truth about death."

"And have you found the truth yet?" I asked.

Sarah shook her head. "My studies haven't provided the answers, only theories. But knowing that Nathan is speaking to you gives me hope."

Seeing as we were being open and honest about things, I decided to confide in Sarah further. "My mum passed away a couple of years ago. She knew there was an afterlife. Near the end, she would talk about it. About who would be there to greet her, and what it would be like. It made me feel better, to think her spirit would continue." I looked up at Sarah who looked a little surprised. I had never mentioned my family to her before, and she had never asked. Just as I had never asked her about hers. I continued. "My dad didn't believe in it though. He felt the same as your family, that when you died, that was it. They used to argue about it sometimes."

I put my fork down, my appetite suddenly gone. I hadn't really thought about my dad in a while. We hadn't parted on good terms after my mother's death, and we hadn't spoken since the funeral.

Sarah put her hand on mine, and squeezed it gently. "I'm so sorry. I never knew. Have you heard from her?"

I shook my head. "No, I only seem to be able to hear and talk to Nathan."

"Have you asked him about your mum? Maybe he can talk to her for you," Sarah suggested.

My heart started thumping. It hadn't occurred to me to do so, but I resolved to ask Nathan when I saw him next. It would be amazing to get a message from my mum. I missed her terribly; she would have been pleased I had gone to university, and that I had made some good friends. I wasn't sure if she would be pleased I was having a weird relationship with a spirit, though.

"I should get back to my essay," Sarah said quietly, interrupting my random thoughts. She picked up her plate and cutlery and took them to the sink. I looked down at my unfinished lasagne and garlic bread. I took my plate to the counter and covered it with a tea towel. Perhaps I'd feel hungry later. Sarah rinsed her dishes, dried her hands and came over to me. We hugged for a moment, then she smiled and left the kitchen.

Feeling both eager to get back to my room, yet reluctant at the same time, I made myself a cup of tea and headed out of the kitchen. I was holding my breath as I turned the handle and entered the room, afraid I would find it empty.

I stepped inside and closed the door behind me. I looked up at the bed, where Nathan was sat waiting for me.

*   *   *

The first time I held her in my arms while she slept, became indelibly etched on my soul. Instead of being an ethereal cloud, hovering, watching, touching her face but not feeling her skin, I could feel her heat, her soft skin, and smell the vanilla scent of her hair. I resisted holding her too tight, not wanting her to awake from her deep sleep, but at the same time I wanted to hold her closer.

I hadn't known about her mother. Or that she wasn't speaking to her father. In all the time I had been watching her, she never spoke about it or thought about it. But it was obviously something that pained her. In the kitchen, after she told Sarah, I asked Marielle's guardian angel why she was talking about it now.

"Because I put the thought in her head," he had replied.

"Why?" I had asked.

"Her father is dying. His guardian angel asked me if I would plant the suggestion that she should contact him, so they can reconcile before his passing."

"But that isn't what just happened. If anything, Marielle only seems to be thinking of the bad things about her father. Why would she contact him?"

"She might not. I will not persuade her to do so. She must decide for herself. A forced reconciliation is worse than none at all."

I watched Marielle sigh in her sleep, almost as though she were responding to my memory. I hadn't said anything when she had come back to her room. In fact, she hadn't said anything either. We had fallen into each other's arms, and had kissed with more passion than I had ever known in my lifetime. She didn't seem to be in the mood to talk, and neither was I.

I wondered if I should tell her what the angel had told me. So she could make amends with her father. But the angel had told me she had to decide for herself. If I made her do it, she might not like me for it.

I sighed too. Knowing so much about what was happening was complicated. But at the same time, I was glad not to be kept in the dark.

I wondered again how many more times I would be able to become human like this. Was there a limited number of times I could do it? Would I eventually have to move on to the other side?

The thought of my time with Marielle being limited made me clutch her tighter, and she wriggled a little in my grasp. I loosened my hold and lay my head on the pillow next to her.

Her scent was intoxicating. I breathed it in deeply and

let myself drift, realising this was the first time I would sleep since I had died a few weeks before.

Chapter Ten

I slept deeply, and when I woke up in Nathan's arms, I felt more complete than I had ever felt before. I turned to face him, and watched him sleep for a few minutes. It was still so surreal. He was here, solid and warm and breathing. I had stopped trying to figure out how it was possible, and decided to just enjoy the sensations instead. As though he could sense my gaze, Nathan's eyes opened, and I could see there was no sleepiness or confusion in them. He smiled.

"Good morning," he said. His deep voice sent shivers right through me. I would never tire of hearing his voice.

"Good morning," I replied. I turned my body around until I was facing him properly. I leaned in to kiss him and I was close to losing myself completely in his embrace when there was a knock at the door.

"Marielle? Are you up? We're going to be late for English Lit again."

I pulled away from Nathan and sighed. "I must have slept through my alarm." I looked into his dark eyes. "Will you be here when I get back?"

He smiled and nodded. He watched from the bed as I jumped up and answered the door. "Hey, Sarah, I know, I know, I slept through my alarm," I said, when she clocked my appearance. "You go on ahead, I will be there in a few minutes." She nodded and left, and I closed the door.

Before I even turned around, I knew he had already left. When I went back to the bed, it was neatly made. There was a note on the pillow, written in an angular cursive.

If you need me, just whisper my name.

I smiled. "I will."

I blinked and snapped out of my daydream state, then threw myself into my morning routine. I was twenty minutes late when I slid into my seat at the back, next to Sarah, and I felt a dark stare coming from the front of the room. I pulled my notebook out and tried to listen to the lecture.

A note slid into my vision onto my notebook. Without glancing at Sarah, I opened the note and read it.

"Did Nathan come back?"

Just reading those words brought goose bumps to my arms and I rubbed them. I knew Nathan was nearby, maybe even reading the words over my shoulder.

I scribbled a response on the paper and slid it back to Sarah. By the sound of her sigh, I knew she was dissatisfied with my reply. Despite my best intentions to concentrate, I spent the rest of the lecture wondering whether or not I should tell Sarah the truth. I thought about our conversation the night before, and decided to speak to Nathan about my mother when I saw him later.

Before I had taken down a single note, everyone was filing out of the classroom.

"Are you okay?"

I put my notebook away before turning to Sarah. "Yes," I said. "I'm fine, honestly. Just being a bit of a space cadet at the moment."

Sarah frowned. "No, you were a space cadet before, there's something different about you right now."

I sighed. "It's difficult to explain. But when I figure out how to, you'll be the first to know."

*   *   *

"Nathan."

I look up at Marielle's guardian angel, sensing something is wrong.

"What is it?"

"He's gone. Her father has passed on to the other side. I received the news from his angel just a moment ago."

I look at Marielle, who is now in another class, pretending to concentrate. I can tell from the look on her face she is on a different plane.

I look back at the angel. "I thought they wanted her to reconcile with him?"

"He had given up. His angel did her best to keep him here, until Marielle decided to contact him, but ultimately, he was ready to go home."

"What should I do? Should I tell her?" I don't like the idea of keeping secrets from Marielle, though being privy to so much information, it is difficult not to.

"There's no need, the police will arrive tomorrow to inform her. Just be there with her, comfort her. It's going to be a rough couple of weeks. She will need to leave university and move back to her dad's house, organise the funeral, sort out his things,"

"Whoa, wait just a second. Shouldn't we wait for Marielle to decide to do all of this?"

"Though there is such a thing as free will, in this case, the course of events seem pretty much set."

I turn my attention back to Marielle again, who has abandoned her note-taking and is twirling her pencil on the desk while staring out of the window.

"Are you sure there's nothing I can do to help her?"

"Yes there is, you can comfort her. Be strong for her. That is all she will need."

"Is it possible for you to get in touch with her mother? She hasn't asked me yet, but I assume she will at some point. She may even ask me about her dad. What should I say?"

"That they are at peace, they are happy, and they are together again."

"That just sounds so vague and general. Have you got anything more specific? So she knows for sure?"

Her guardian angel is quiet for a while. "Tell her that when they met on the other side, her father said to her mother – "You were right, Snowdrop. I'm so sorry I doubted you."

I must appear confused to the angel, who adds, "Marielle will understand, and she will know what you say is true."

$$* \qquad * \qquad *$$

The rest of the day passed in a fuzzy haze, and I found myself back in the dorm kitchen. I was halfway through making beans on toast before I even noticed I was doing so. I became aware just in time to save the toast from burning but not in time to save the beans from sticking to the bottom of the pan.

I served up my very student-like meal and put the pan in the sink to soak.

I had just sat down when Sarah came in. I greeted her but she didn't respond. Instead, she put the kettle on and made herself a drink. Still in uncharacteristic silence, she picked up her mug and came over to the table. She sat down across from me, but didn't say a word. I stopped eating and looked up.

"Are you okay?" I asked, breaking the weird energy surrounding us.

She nodded. "I was just waiting for you to find a way to explain."

I sighed. "Oh, I see." I shrugged and picked up my fork again. "I still haven't figured it out, in all honesty."

"You could start with the basic stuff," Sarah said. I could see the curiosity mixed with concern in her eyes. "Like what it's like when Nathan visits, and what he says. Could I read what you've written?"

"What I've written?" I repeated, forgetting that as far as Sarah knew, the only way Nathan and I communicated was through automatic writing.

Sarah frowned. "That is how you're talking to him, isn't it?"

"Yes, um, it was in the beginning. But now I just talk to him out loud, and I uh, hear his reply in my mind."

Sarah's eyes widened. "So the connection is getting stronger?"

You have no idea, I thought to myself. I nodded a little, and stuffed some food in my mouth so I wouldn't have to speak.

"Is he here now? Can you ask him some questions for me?"

Damn. Hadn't thought that lie through when I'd said it. Maybe I could just say he wasn't here.

I'm here.

I jumped a little, making Sarah jump too. I had heard his voice. In my ear, as clear as day. "Uh, uh," I stammered, suddenly thrown by this new development. "Yes, he's here."

"You can hear him?"

I nodded. "Yes. But perhaps we should move this conversation into one of our rooms." Just at that moment, Susie came into the kitchen with a glazed look on her face. In need of her Diet Coke fix, no doubt.

Sarah nodded too, then jumped up and headed for the door. I followed her more slowly, feeling a bit weird about being the go-between for her and Nathan.

It'll be fine.

I jumped again as I heard Nathan's voice in my ear. I headed out of the door, not even bothering to say hello to Susie, as she rummaged through the fridge. She seemed to be completely oblivious to my existence anyway.

I knocked on Sarah's door, and it opened a second later. I went in and took up my usual spot on her desk chair while she bounced, cross-legged on the bed.

There was a pause, and a ripple of goose bumps went up and down my body, making my hair stand up uncomfortably.

"What did you want to ask? I'll try to translate," I said, shifting to get comfortable in the chair.

"You mean he's speaking a different language?" Sarah asked.

I chuckled and I heard Nathan's laughter too. "No, I just meant, never mind, what are your questions?"

Sarah was thoughtful for a while, then she smiled. "Can you ask him what happens when you die? Is it painful? Is there a light? Do you know you are dead? Are you greeted by your family when you get there? Is it–"

"Whoa!" I held up my hand. "I think perhaps we should go a little more slowly. Let's just do the first question, shall we?"

Sarah nodded and waited. For no reason, I closed my eyes, as if it would make it easier for me to hear Nathan's words. As he began to speak, I repeated his words softly.

*   *   *

Though Sarah's interrogation didn't last very long, Marielle was exhausted by the time she returned to her room. I was already waiting for her in bed when she had finished in the bathroom. Despite her tiredness, her eyes lit up when she saw me.

"I'm so sorry," she said, sliding under the covers next to me. "I had no idea she would ask me to do that." The last word was drawn out in a yawn, and she snuggled into my arms. Her eyes closed and within seconds, before I could even respond to her apology, she was fast asleep.

I watched her for a while, glad in a way we'd not had time to speak properly. I was dreading the next day, dreading the news I knew was coming to her. I lay there awake all night, just watching her, and waiting for the dawn. Time seemed to go so slowly compared to when I was in my ethereal form. It appeared I didn't really need sleep, even while human. And I didn't need to eat or drink, though I think I could. Clothes didn't seem to be a problem either, they just appeared on my body in response to how I felt I should be clothed.

When the sun finally appeared, casting a pink glow through the window, I felt relieved. The sooner today was over, the better.

A couple of hours later, Marielle stirred in my arms. Her alarm went off twice before it really had any effect on her. I kissed her cheek and she smiled in her sleep. She really was beautiful, even first thing in the morning.

I kissed her again, and this time she turned her head and kissed me back.

"Good morning," she whispered. "Did you sleep okay?"

I shook my head. "No, but I don't really need to. Did you sleep well?"

She nodded and stretched her arms above her head, hitting her fists on the wall. The bed was bricked in, and wasn't really big enough for two people. It was a good thing she wasn't a star-sleeper.

"I guess I should get up," she murmured. "It would be nice to stay here with you though."

I leaned down and kissed her again, wishing we could just stay in bed. But a minute later there was a knock at the door.

Marielle groaned. "Talk about déjà vu," she whispered. She reached up to kiss me and smiled. "Will you be here later?"

I nodded, unable to speak for fear I would say something I wasn't supposed to. I watched her get out of bed and wrap a dressing gown around herself. Before she opened the door, I re-entered the angel dimension.

*   *   *

"Marielle!"

"What?"

Sarah looked frantic. "There's two police officers in the kitchen. They're looking for you."

Even though I had not done anything wrong - that I knew of - my heart started hammering. I had always had a bit of a guilty conscience, and now my mind was thrown into a whir of trying to figure out why the police were looking for me.

"What do they want?" I hissed, pulling my dressing gown tighter.

Sarah shook her head. "I don't know, they won't tell me anything. Do you want me to stay with you?"

I nodded quickly. "Yes, please, just let me get some clothes on." I retreated into my room, noticing that Nathan had gone. I threw on yesterday's clothes and sprayed myself with some deodorant. I ran a brush through my hair and took some slow, deep breaths, and tried to calm myself, but my imagination was running wild.

I had never been in trouble before, what could they possibly want with me?

Within five minutes, I was outside in the corridor, and Sarah gave me a reassuring smile. Heart still hammering, the sound of it thudding in my ears, we walked to the kitchen together. My stomach was churning, and I felt like I might throw up.

When I saw the two uniformed officers, one male and one female, their grave expressions made my heart stop.

"Marielle Gibson?" the male officer asked, standing up from his seat at the kitchen table.

I nodded mutely, and Sarah gave my arm a reassuring squeeze before crossing the room to put the kettle on.

"I'm Officer Harris and this is Officer Hadley. Would you like to sit down?" He gestured to an empty seat at the table and I nodded again, noting that his voice seemed quite gentle. It didn't sound like I was in trouble, so what did they want?

I sat at the table and Sarah put a cup of tea in front of me. I took a tiny sip, wincing at the sweetness. She must have thought I was in shock, which I suppose in a way, I was. Sarah sat next to me and Officer Harris sat back down.

"I'm afraid we have some bad news for you," Officer Hadley started, her own voice rougher than Officer Harris', but her tone soft.

"Bad news?" I repeated. I set the mug down on the table and tried to focus on her face. I felt Sarah's arm around my shoulders.

"Your father has been very ill in hospital for the last week, and unfortunately, he passed away yesterday."

I blinked several times, and tried to process her words.

"My father. Ill. Dead?" My incoherence didn't seem to surprise them at all, I felt Sarah squeeze me tighter, but everything had become a little fuzzy.

"I'm very sorry. Apparently he told the hospital he had no next of kin, so they didn't inform you. It was only after he passed that they found a letter in his things, addressed to you. They informed us and asked us to find you."

I blinked a few more times, none of her words stuck, but the meaning was clear. He hadn't wanted to see me. The stubborn man had been on his deathbed, and he hadn't wanted to see me. At that thought, the tears began. Several rolled down my cheeks, blurring my vision further, but I didn't know what to say.

Sarah spoke for me. "What happens now?"

"As the only next of kin, it's down to Marielle to make the funeral arrangements," Officer Harris replied. He took a letter out from his jacket pocket and slid it across the table to me. I looked down, and wiped away some tears so I could read the envelope. My name and address was on it, in my dad's handwriting.

"What does it say?" I asked, unable to bring myself to pick it up.

"We haven't opened it, we have only used the information on the envelope to find you."

My hands were shaking, but I managed to open it, and unfold the single sheet of paper inside.

It was brief, and to the point. He was sorry we had fallen out, and he wished me a happy future. He also said he had a will, and he had left everything to me. He listed the details of his solicitor, and the numbers of all the utility providers for the house. I read the words a second time, looking for some kind of sentiment, some tiny bit of love that had gone into the words, but there was none. He had even signed it with his name, instead of 'Dad'.

I set the letter down and looked up at the officers. "So I need to arrange the funeral?" They both nodded.

"Do you have transportation? We can arrange that if necessary," Officer Harris said.

I shook my head. "I have my car. Thank you."

There were a few moments of silence, and the officers shifted in their seats slightly. I could tell they were feeling a little uncomfortable now.

I stood up, and wobbled a little. Sarah stood up too and put a supportive arm around my waist. The officers stood as well.

Officer Hadley held out a card. "If you need any assistance, this is my number. And on the back is the number of the person you need to speak to at the hospital. They should be able to advise you on what to do next."

I nodded, and brushed a few more tears away. "Thank you."

They both nodded, and made their way out of the kitchen. I slumped back into the chair.

Without saying a word, Sarah wrapped both of her arms around me and held me tight. I didn't know how to feel. My tears had stopped and I was staring unseeingly at the noticeboard on the wall. The words and colours of the posters pinned there blurred and moved, making no sense to me at all.

Sarah pulled back a little to look at me. "Are you okay?" she whispered, watching my face closely. I looked at her, and blinked a few times to focus on her face.

"I don't know," I said honestly. "I think I need to go lie down for a bit. I can't quite process it all."

She nodded and let me go. "I'm right here when you need me, I'm not going to my classes today. Would you like me to bring you another cup of tea in a bit?"

I nodded, and picked up the letter and my barely

touched cup of ultra-sweet tea. I took a sip, then headed out of the room. I walked back to my room without blinking, without thinking, without noticing anything around me. How I didn't spill my tea everywhere, I didn't know. I could barely feel the warm mug in my hands.

I opened my door and stepped into the room. I managed to set the mug down on the bedside table, and the letter next to it, before sitting on my bed. I sensed his presence a moment before I heard his voice.

*　　　*　　　*

"Marielle," I whispered. She looked up at me. Her tear-stained face and confused, heartbroken expression tore open my heart. Before I could reach for her, her expression changed, and she looked at me almost accusingly.

"Did you know?" she asked.

I froze in place, unable to move. I couldn't lie to her, but at the same time, could I bear the look on her face when she realised I'd known, and not said anything?

I swallowed, but couldn't get past the giant lump in my throat.

"I knew last night, that he had gone," I whispered. I stayed where I was, afraid to move closer to her.

Her face fell, and a tear rolled down her cheek. "Why didn't you tell me?"

I sighed. "I wanted to, but I was told not to. I was told all I could do was be here for you."

She nodded and her face crumpled. A sob escaped from her, and the sound broke me out of my frozen state. I went to her and sat next to her on the bed. I gathered her up in my arms and she sobbed into my shoulder.

I held her shaking body for a long time, and tried to soothe her with soft words, but nothing seemed to calm her.

I thought about telling her what her angel had said to me, but I didn't know if it would make the situation better or worse. Before I could decide, there was a knock at the door.

"Marielle?" It was Sarah. Marielle lifted her head, her red, puffy eyes blinked hard. She looked at me and shook her head.

"I don't want to see her right now, can you tell her to go?"

I frowned. "I don't know if I can. I'm not sure she can see me."

Marielle frowned too. I don't think it had occurred to her that perhaps she was the only one who could see me. In fact, it hadn't occurred to me whether that was true either.

Our state of confusion went on for a few seconds and there was another knock at the door, only this one was followed a few seconds later by the door opening. Marielle removed herself from my arms and stood up, as if to shield me from Sarah, but there was no need, I was already back in the angel dimension.

*   *   *

I look up at her angel, who is right next to her. "Is that how it works? Is Marielle the only one who can see me?"

"It would seem that way," her angel replies. "Though it could just be your own beliefs that cause you to slip back into this realm when anyone else is around."

I think about this. Do I believe no one else can see me? Or is it that I don't want anyone else but Marielle to see me?

Sarah stays with Marielle for the rest of the day, refusing

to leave her alone. I stay there too, just in case. In the early evening, Sarah finally leaves, after Marielle insists she is alright, and doesn't want any dinner.

While Marielle is in the bathroom, I feel myself entering the physical realm again, this time dressed for bed.

*   *   *

The bathroom light clicked off, and Marielle came back into the room. She sighed in relief when she saw me sitting on her bed.

"I'm so glad you're here," she whispered, moving toward me. I helped her get into bed, and got in beside her, wrapping my arms around her when I felt her shivering. She snuggled into my embrace, and within a few moments the shivering stopped and her breathing slowed.

"Sleep," I whispered. "I'll be right here when you wake."

She nodded into my chest, and her body relaxed into mine. I lay awake that night too. I couldn't help but wonder whether my dad had comforted my mum in this way, when I had died. I hoped so.

Chapter Eleven

The moment before I opened my eyes the next morning, the events of the previous day rushed back to me. I held back a sob, and tried to breathe deeply. My father was dead. I breathed in a few breaths, trying to allow that knowledge to sink in. I really didn't know how to feel. My chest ached from crying most of yesterday, and I felt a little hollow inside.

"Hey."

I opened my eyes as far as I could, they were like slits from the puffiness. I looked up into Nathan's dark eyes and tried to smile.

"Hey," I echoed.

Without another word, he tilted my chin up and kissed me softly. "I'm so sorry I didn't tell you. It's so hard, knowing so much from being in the other dimension, yet not being able to say anything, because if I did, I would be messing with free will or destiny or whatever."

I blinked and rubbed my tired, bleary eyes. "It's okay." The words were out of my mouth before I'd even thought of what to say. But I realised the truth in them. It really was okay. Because even if Nathan had told me the night before, it wouldn't have mattered. It still would have been too late to say goodbye to my father.

I could see Nathan was relieved I wasn't mad at him. I lifted a hand to stroke his stubbly cheek. "I'm just glad you're with me right now," I whispered.

He nodded and kissed me again. I kissed him back, and tears squeezed out of my swollen eyes and rolled down my cheeks.

He pulled back. "I promise I will help you through this."

I nodded, and before I dissolved into sobs again, I pulled away and got out of bed. Nathan watched me slip my dressing gown on and disappear into the bathroom. I switched the light on and the whirring fan came to life. I looked at my swollen, puffy face in the mirror and sighed. There was so much to figure out, so much to do, and I couldn't just hide under the covers and pretend none of it existed. I had a funeral to arrange, a whole house of stuff to sort out, how could I possibly keep up with my studies as well?

I splashed cold water onto my face before brushing my teeth. It felt as though my mind was whirring as loudly as the bathroom fan. Before making any concrete decisions, I figured it would be a good idea to see my course tutor, and ask her what she thought I should do.

Feeling a little better at having made at least one decision, I slipped my clothes off and stepped into the shower. As the hot water pounded down onto me, I let all thought go.

*   *   *

She was coping better than I'd imagined she would. I lay in her bed, listening to the sound of the shower running. I should have known she would be able to deal with it, she was pretty strong really. I remembered her reaction to the news of my death. What was running through her mind right now? Did she think that because I had come back from the dead, her father would too? Or even her mother? The words of her guardian angel came back to me and I repeated them softly to myself. I would have to tell her at the right moment, when she was ready for the reassurance that both her parents were happy and together again.

The shower stopped, and I heard the curtain scrape back. I got up from the bed and closed my eyes, setting the intention to be dressed. When I opened my eyes, I was dressed. I sat on Marielle's desk chair, and waited for her to emerge from the shower. I wondered if I should leave, and give her some space, but I also wanted her to know I was there to support her.

A few minutes later, she stepped out of the tiny en-suite, wrapped in a pink towel. She saw me sat at her desk, and seemed surprised.

"You're still here."

I smiled. "Yes, I wasn't sure whether to leave and give you some space, but I didn't want to just disappear while you were in the bathroom."

She nodded. "I'll be fine for a bit. I'm going to get dressed and go to see my course tutor. I need to find out what my options are if I have to take some time off to go and sort my dad's stuff out."

I was surprised. It sounded like she already had it all figured out. "Okay, I'll leave for a bit. But if at any point you need me, just say my name. I won't be too far away."

I crossed the room and pulled her into a damp hug. She wrapped her arms around me and buried her head in my chest. "Thank you," she whispered.

After a few moments, I released her. When she turned away from me, I melted back into the angelic dimension.

*   *   *

"You handled that beautifully."

I look at Marielle's guardian angel. "It still feels a bit wrong, not telling her I knew he was going to die. That I could have warned her so she could have at least called him or something."

"I know. But this is the way it has worked out, therefore it is the right way. Nothing is ever 'wrong' or 'bad'. It is all part of the perfection that is life."

If I had physical eyebrows I'd be raising them at this point. "The perfection that is life? Life may be many things, but it's certainly not perfect."

"Do you honestly believe God would create anything that is not perfect?"

"Of course. That's why there is death and disease and war and poverty."

"Ah," the guardian angel said. "You have confused the word perfect with the word good. All that is perfect may not be good. Because there is perfection in what humans see as good and bad. Perfect is neither positive nor negative, it is all encompassing. Everything that happens is perfect, everything that exists is perfect. Every person is perfect. If it was not perfect, it would not exist."

I let his words flow through me. The more human part of me wants to argue the point. But my soul agrees with him. The part of me that is more connected to divinity than to earth is ethereally nodding in agreement with his words.

"I can see what you are saying. But why is it you can see the perfection, but humans cannot?"

"Because that is the reason why they are human. Every soul on the planet knows, at a soul level, of this perfection, of the oneness that is life, yet they have been asked to forget, they have been asked to live as though there is such a thing as imperfection and lack and hate and anger."

"But why would they be asked to do this? What is the

point?"

The guardian angel smiles at me. "Who said there had to be one?"

*   *   *

By lunchtime, I knew what I had to do. Though my course tutor had tried to reassure me that I could take a couple of weeks off, and still catch up again with the coursework, there was a voice inside my head (that wasn't Nathan) that suggested perhaps it would just be putting too much strain on me. It would be best to just quit the course now and move back to my father's house. I had been to the accommodation office, and they had even said they would be able to refund part of my money, because they had a waiting list of people waiting for a dorm room. Though I had wanted to get my degree, and had been so excited when I had got into university, suddenly it all seemed a bit pointless.

I was staring into space, holding my cold cup of tea, when I heard someone enter the kitchen. A moment later I felt a hand on my shoulder.

"Hey," Sarah said. "I knocked on your door this morning, but there was no answer. How are you?"

"I went to see my course tutor. To see what to do." I looked up at Sarah. "I've decided to leave the course."

Sarah's face fell and she sat down in the chair opposite me. "Surely you can just take some time off and come back in a few weeks? Did she really say you have to quit?"

I shook my head. "No, she didn't. She was keen for me to stay on the course. But I just know that once I leave here, and go back to the house, I won't want to come back."

Sarah frowned. "Why not? You have friends here, you

were enjoying the course. What is there that would keep you there?"

It had occurred to me earlier in the day that if I lived in my dad's cottage in the middle of nowhere, Nathan wouldn't have to keep disappearing all the time. He could stay with me permanently, without being found out by anyone. But I couldn't tell Sarah that the reason I would want to stay would be so my ghost boyfriend could be with me all the time.

I shrugged. "It's just a feeling I have, I can't explain it." I could tell by her expression she wasn't entirely convinced by my vague lie, but I was too exhausted to care.

I stood up and took my cup to the sink, tipping the cold tea away. "Do you want a cuppa?"

"Yes, please."

I put the kettle on to boil again and got her favourite mug out. My actions were so automatic that it suddenly hit me how I was so used to having Sarah around. A tear fell and splashed onto the counter. I looked at her, sat at the table, her shoulders slumped. I would miss her. She had become a close friend, and until Nathan had appeared, we had kept very few secrets from one another. Without thinking about it, I crossed the room to where she sat and wrapped my arms around her from behind.

"I'll miss you," I said, hugging her tightly. "I'm sorry we won't be neighbours anymore, but I know I need to do this."

I felt her tears hitting my hands. "I know. I'm going to miss you too. But I know you're doing what's right for you."

We hugged for a long time. The kettle clicked off and neither of us moved. By the time I pulled away, I needed to boil the kettle again.

*   *   *

Though time has lost most of its meaning, it seems like everything has sped up suddenly. I watch Marielle sort things out with her course tutor and the admin office, then I watch Sarah help her pack up her belongings and put them in the car. She has already called the hospital and informed them she is going to be there in the next couple of days to make the arrangements for the funeral. It seems like only an hour or two later when she is standing by her car, saying goodbye to Sarah. I know they have a deep bond, and when I mention it to her guardian angel, she confirms that their friendship has run through several lifetimes previously. Which is why they see through each other's lies.

After a final tearful hug, Marielle gets into her car and pulls away. She only looks in the rear-view mirror once at Sarah, who is still standing out in the cold, hugging herself.

When she is a few miles away from the university, on the country lanes where it is unlikely she will pass anyone she knows, I re-enter the earthly realm.

*   *   *

I reached across from the passenger side to place my hand on her knee. She kept her eyes trained on the road, but a tear rolled down her cheek.

"I'm here," I whispered. "Everything's going to be okay."

She nodded but didn't say a word. For the next four hours, she kept her eyes glued to the road. I tried to start up a conversation a couple of times, but realised she just needed quiet in order to build herself up for the tough few days ahead. I relaxed into the silence, and just squeezed her knee every now and then, in what I hoped was a reassuring manner.

When we finally turned into the lane, and pulled up in front of the tiny cottage, I realised my body felt stiff from being stuffed into the tiny space for too long. Aches and pains were a foreign feeling to me, it felt like such a long time since I'd felt anything like it. Even though I had only died a few weeks before.

She turned off the engine and stared at the house for a while. It was dark now, and we could only see the outline of the building in the faint moonlight filtering through the trees.

"My mum loved this place. My dad wasn't so sure. He liked living on the coast. He liked swimming in the sea through the summer. But my mum craved the quiet, she hated putting up with all of the tourists. I'm surprised my dad stayed here after she died. I thought he would sell up and move away."

Though her voice was barely above a whisper, in the absolute dead silence it seemed quite loud. I rubbed her leg. "You don't have to stay here tonight, we could go and find a B&B or a hotel or something, come back tomorrow, in the daylight."

She shook her head, her eyes still fixed on the front door. "No, it's okay. I need to do it now." She got out of the car, and I followed her. I stretched out my limbs, and closed my eyes momentarily to set the intention for the aches to melt away. As I joined her, I felt the tension in my body dissolve.

With a deep breath, Marielle walked up the path to the front door. She reached under the mat and pulled out a key. "You would have thought he would have removed this, knowing he was probably not coming home from the hospital."

"Perhaps he didn't have time to," I suggested. Marielle nodded and put the key in the lock and turned it. We stepped into the cottage, which smelled a little damp from not having the heating on for a while. She flicked a switch in the front hallway and a gloomy energy-saving bulb flickered on, barely lighting up the cluttered space.

Marielle made her way into the kitchen, and her gasp when she turned on the light prepared me for the sight of quite possibly the messiest kitchen I had ever seen. She shook her head.

"He was never keen on washing up, but this is beyond ridiculous." She took a few steps in, stepping on the rubbish strewn on the floor. She looked back at me and her forlorn expression was enough to make me step toward her and envelop her in a hug.

"We'll sort it out, it'll be fine, you'll see."

*   *   *

The next few days were anything but fine. I made so many phone calls and made so many arrangements, that everything began to blur together and make no sense anymore. Cleaning and sorting the house seemed to be taking forever, and I frequently found myself thanking God for sending Nathan back to me, because there was just no way I could have coped with it all by myself.

On the morning of the funeral, I found myself lying in bed next to Nathan, staring at the ceiling which had a nasty-looking damp patch on it, wondering how on earth my life had turned out this way. And what would happen after today? Once my last remaining family member was buried, what should I do?

"Morning," Nathan whispered in my ear.

I opened my eyes and looked up at him. "Morning."

"Are you okay?"

I shook my head. If I tried to speak, I knew I would just end up sobbing. And I needed to get through the day without having a complete breakdown.

Nathan pulled me tighter to him, and his hug both comforted me and made me stronger. "Let's do this," I whispered. I felt his agreeing nod, and without any more words, we both got up and got ready for the funeral. My preference for black clothing came in handy, as I had more than enough choices of outfits for the occasion. But on top of the sombre, black ensemble, I added a bright red scarf. It was my dad's favourite colour, and also one of the last Christmas presents he had given me. It was only a small gesture, but it made me feel closer to him.

After I had eaten breakfast, Nathan and I got in my car and drove to the crematorium. I had put a notice in the local paper about dad's passing, and I had contacted a few old family friends, but I wasn't hopeful many would turn up.

Outside the small, simple building, I parked the car and switched off the engine. I looked over at Nathan, who just seemed too big to be in such a tiny car.

"Will you stay with me?"

Nathan nodded. "I'm always with you. But I think it would be best if I weren't visible."

"Why? There's not really going to be anyone in there, and does it matter if the vicar sees you? We'll probably never see him again." I had been against having a religious service at first. My dad was not a religious person, and neither was I. But when faced with the choice between a vicar doing a short service and doing it myself, I had opted for the vicar.

"I know, but, well…" Nathan was stalling, I could see he was trying to come up with a good reason why he shouldn't be seen by anyone else, but he couldn't. "I'll stay with you," he said finally. Relief flooded through me. I really didn't want to go through the service alone.

I got out of the car and Nathan followed suit. He had just reached my side when the hearse arrived. Before I could stop it, a tear rolled down my cheek. Nathan tightened his grip on my hand, and we watched silently as the coffin was removed from the hearse. Adorning the simple wooden box was a bunch of lilies. I had chosen them only because it was the wrong time of year for snowdrops, which were my parents' favourite flower, and also, my dad's nickname for my mum. The men from the funeral parlour carried the coffin into the crematorium, and with a deep breath, I followed, Nathan firmly by my side. We entered the quiet room, and the only sound was our muffled footsteps on the carpet. We sat in the front row, and I stared at the coffin. I knew I should have found some music to play for the funeral, but I couldn't find any CDs amongst the mess and clutter, and there didn't seem to be anything in the house to play music on anyway. After my mum died, I think my dad had given up on having anything joyful in the house again. So a silent funeral seemed fitting in a way, if not a little depressing.

"Are we waiting for anyone else?" The vicar's soft voice in my ear made me jump, and I turned to look into his kind eyes. I looked around at the room, empty except for the three of us, and I shook my head.

"No, it's just us two."

The vicar smiled gently and nodded. He didn't even look at Nathan, and I wondered if he was actually able to see him, or whether it just looked like I was holding an invisible hand.

The vicar went to the small podium, and I whispered to Nathan. "Can he see you?"

"No," Nathan whispered back. "I don't think he can."

I nodded, and the vicar took that to be his cue to begin his short sermon. I had given him a few details about my father, but I didn't really feel like there was much to say. Everything I had wanted to say was to him. Not to this empty room. Ignoring the vicar completely, I began talking to my dad in my mind.

Dad, I am so sorry I didn't come to see you, I'm so sorry we weren't talking, and hadn't done for so long. A tear fell, and I blinked. *I forgive you, Dad. For all the pain, for all the arguments. I know you loved me, I loved you too. I just hope you're at peace now, and with Mum.*

I bowed my head and squeezed Nathan's hand. He leaned close to me, and whispered in my ear.

"There's something I forgot to tell you. When your father passed over to the light, he was met by your mother. And he said to her: 'You were right, Snowdrop. I'm so sorry I doubted you'."

I turned to look at Nathan, and I knew why God had sent him back to me. Though my heart was aching, and part of me wanted to break down and sob for what I had lost, I was so very thankful for what I had.

I smiled at Nathan, and he looked a little surprised at my reaction. "Thank you," I whispered. I turned back to the vicar, who was wrapping up with a prayer. He seemed surprised at my smile too. I couldn't explain why I suddenly felt happy. Nathan's words had brought me such a strong feeling of peace. And I knew everything would be alright.

*　　　*　　　*

The funeral passed by quickly, which was probably a good thing. If Marielle had kept talking to me, and therefore appear to be talking to herself, the good vicar might just have been making some calls at the end of the day to have her locked up.

Back at the tiny cottage, Marielle put the kettle on and made herself a cup of tea. She was staring out of the window, hands wrapped tightly around the chipped mug. I wrapped my arms around her, and she leaned her head back onto my shoulder.

"I can't believe not a single other person came to his funeral. What has he been doing these last few years? Has he just been here, on his own? I don't even know what he was doing for work, or how he was supporting himself."

"Will you be meeting with the solicitor about his will?"

"Yes, he's next on my list of people to call. I just needed to get the funeral out of the way first." She turned to face me. "How did you know what he said to my mum when he crossed over?"

I smiled. "Your guardian angel told me."

Marielle frowned. "But you are my guardian angel."

I laughed and shook my head. "No, I'm not. I'm just a guy who you used to go to school with, who died then came back to haunt you. Your guardian angel has been with you from the moment you were born. And is with you in every moment of your life, looking out for you, guiding you, protecting you and keeping you safe."

Marielle thought for a moment. "Does everyone have one?"

"Of course they do. Angels do not discriminate."

"Where was yours? Why did they let you die?"

I sighed. "I had this same conversation with your angel. Apparently, I had already decided on when I would pass over, before I was born. Everything happened exactly as it should."

"So it was just your time?"

"Yes. It was."

"But if it was your time, how come you've come back?" Marielle took a sip of her tea. "If we were meant to be together, wouldn't it have been better if you had carried on living?"

I shook my head. "I have no idea." A thought gripped me, one I had been pushing away for a while, but kept arising. "Have you thought that perhaps we weren't meant to be together?"

Marielle stepped back, looking like I had just stabbed her in the heart. "What?" she whispered.

I bit my lip. This really wasn't the best time to be discussing this, and I knew it. "I'm sorry, it's nothing, forget it."

"No, I can't just forget it. You don't think we should be together?"

I sighed. I really should have kept my mouth shut. "I just don't see how we can be, properly. I mean, you're the only person who can see me. Which means we can never go out together in public. We can't do anything a normal couple can do. We can't get married, have kids, and grow old together. I'm not human anymore. I don't know what I am, but I know I can't give you everything you need or want."

Marielle set her mug down on the counter. "I think I need to be on my own for a bit. Could you go?"

I wasn't expecting her to react like that. But perhaps it was a good thing. I nodded. "Just call me when you want me to return."

Marielle turned away and looked back out of the window, and I took her silence to be an agreement.

*   *   *

I re-enter the angel realm, my human body disappears, and my form becomes free and fluid once again. I see her guardian angel, he has his wings enveloped around her, and is whispering into her ear. I know his words of comfort will ease her pain.

I move away, needing to give her space and time to herself. I'll hear her call through our bond, no matter how far away I am.

In this state, I feel no regret or sadness for what has just transpired, but I do have a million questions. With a thought, I move to my favourite beach. I watch the waves crashing on the rocks, and see the winds blowing through the bunting adorning the pathways along the promenade. I love the sea. There is something calming about it. I allow myself to run the questions through my mind, and I wait for the answers to arrive on the breeze, in the way I know they will.

*   *   *

As weird as it felt, to be alone in the cottage without him, I knew I needed to process all that was happening. I felt as though I had gone from one extreme to another. From needing Nathan's touch and his comfort, to needing to be completely alone. Though according to Nathan, that was impossible, as my guardian angel was always with me.

I threw myself into sorting the house out. I filled bag after bag of rubbish, clothing and clutter. I arranged a meeting with my dad's solicitor, who had a copy of his will. I also arranged meetings with his bank. The sooner I found out the reality of the financial situation, the sooner I could work out what to do next.

Without really remembering the drive there, I found myself in the tiny but immaculately clean and tidy office of

Mr Warren. I shifted in the uncomfortable chair, and waited for him to get all of the papers out.

"It's quite simple, Ms Gibson. Your father left everything to you. His savings, possessions and the house. Which is free and clear, and all yours."

I nodded. "I'm going to the bank soon to find out what the situation is there. So that's it? The house and its contents are mine. He didn't put anything else in there?"

Mr Warren smiled. "There were no notes or anything. He changed his will after your mother passed away, and I haven't seen him since."

"Okay. Thank you."

"I will get the papers in order to transfer the deeds of the property into your name, then you will be free to sell it if you wish."

"I haven't decided what to do yet. Whether or not to stay."

"Give yourself time, I'm sure you will make the right decision." Mr Warren stood up, and I took that as my cue to leave. I shook his hand and left his office, stepping out into the chilly breeze.

Though tiny, the village was a busy one, and people walked by me as I stood outside the office, wondering what to do now. The idea of going back to the empty cottage just seemed too depressing to contemplate. Instead, I headed for the village's only café.

I stepped into the cosy warmth, instantly feeling better. I nabbed a table for two toward the back, away from the door.

"Can I take your order?"

I looked up into the smiling face of the waitress, holding a notepad and pen and wearing an old-fashioned frilly apron.

I blinked. "Um, a latte, please."

She didn't even bother to write it down. Instead she tucked the notepad into her apron pocket and nodded. "Anything else?"

I shook my head, and she left. I dug around in my handbag and got my phone out. There was no reception at the cottage, and it was only marginally better here. There were several text messages from Sarah. I sighed. I felt bad for not keeping in touch, I really should call her. I looked around and saw that the few people in the café were all occupied with chatting or reading books and newspapers. I decided to call Sarah once I had my drink.

"Here you go, a large latte. And I thought you looked like you needed some of this." The waitress placed a generous slice of chocolate cake in front of me.

I smiled up at her. "Thank you, I think I do need that."

She smiled back and returned to the kitchen. I ate a mouthful of cake, which was seriously good, before scrolling through my phone contacts for Sarah's number.

It only rang once.

"Marielle! Are you okay? What's going on? Why didn't you ring me? I don't even have an address for you. I was so worried!"

If I felt bad before, I felt even worse now.

"Sarah, I'm so sorry. It's just been so crazy, trying to sort out the funeral and the house was a complete state. I haven't really been out much and there's absolutely zero reception at the cottage. But there is a landline, I'll text you the number later."

"It's okay, I'm just so glad you're alright. I was really worried."

"I know, I should have been in touch, it's just been hard getting my head around everything."

"How did it go? The funeral?"

I sighed. "As well as it possibly could. I was the only

one there."

"You're kidding me? Oh, honey, I would have come and been with you if I'd known. You shouldn't have had to do that alone."

I thought of Nathan and felt bad for saying I had been alone, when I hadn't, not at all. I'd had the comfort of the most amazing soul I had ever met. And I had pushed him away.

"–would that be okay?"

I blinked and brought my attention back to the conversation. "Would what be okay? Sorry I totally zoned out for a moment."

"I want to come and visit you soon. If it's okay with you."

I smiled. "Yes that would be lovely, though I'm not sure how much longer I will stay in the cottage. I was thinking it might be best to sell it. I could use the money to buy a place closer to a town or city. It's pretty quiet around here."

"Sounds like it could be a good idea. After all, there must be a lot of memories in that house."

"Yes, and not very good ones, either."

"I have to go now, I'm late for class. But please call me again, and make sure you text me the house number. There's so much we need to catch up on."

"I will," I promised. "It was good to talk to you. I won't leave it so long next time."

"You'd better not! Love you."

"Love you too." I hung up the phone and ate some more chocolate cake. After a few moments, I got the feeling someone was staring at me, and I looked over to see the waitress watching me. Instead of being embarrassed at being caught, she just smiled and continued filling the sugar dispensers.

I stared out through the window. My thoughts drifted

away from the waitress back to Nathan. I missed him. I missed his touch, his embrace, his voice. As hurt as I had been, I understood his concern, his fears that I would miss out on normal things we couldn't do. But I didn't think it was wrong for us to be together. In fact, nothing else in my life had ever felt so right.

Unable to spend another moment without him, I finished my latte and cake quickly, then motioned for the bill. The waitress brought it over, and I realised she hadn't charged me for the cake. I left a decent tip to say thank you, gathered my things and stepped out into chilly air again.

I hurried back to my car and drove the few miles back to the cottage in silence. I resisted calling to Nathan while I drove, wanting to be in the safety and privacy of the house before I spoke to him.

I parked badly, clipping the stones edging the grass. I turned off the engine and hurried inside, not even bothering to lock the car. The chance of it being stolen here was so remote, it seemed like a waste of time.

Once inside the house, I put the kettle on, needing a cup of tea, not because I was thirsty, but because for some reason, I was really nervous and needed to occupy myself.

While I poured the hot water onto the tea bag, I finally let myself call out to Nathan in my mind.

I didn't have to wait long for him to appear.

*   *   *

"I'm here."

Marielle turned to face me, and it took all my strength and willpower not to cross the room in two strides and wrap her in my arms. She looked particularly fragile in that moment, and it made my heart ache.

"Thank you for coming back," she said softly.

"I said I would. I wasn't too far away. With our bond, I'm never very far away."

She smiled. "I'm sorry I asked you to go. I've missed you."

I couldn't stop myself any longer. Within seconds, I had her in my arms and was breathing in the warm, vanilla scent of her hair. "I missed you too."

"Where were you?"

"Hanging out with the angels. I visited the seaside too. There's something about being near the sea that helps me to think clearly. Even now. I guess some things don't change when you die."

"Do you still feel we shouldn't be together?"

I could hear the fear in her voice, and it made me feel bad. "No. Now I've had time to think, and to talk to the angels about it, I realise how silly I was to think that. If we weren't meant to be together, me being here just wouldn't be possible."

"Why is that?"

"Because your guardian angel wouldn't allow it."

Marielle pulled back a little to look up at me. "You think he would have stopped you if he didn't think this was a good idea?"

"I know he would have. He wants only what is for your highest good. He would have stopped the whole thing ages ago if it was wrong. But instead, he's been helping it to happen. So therefore I need to trust that he knows what he's doing."

Marielle was quiet for a while, then she pulled away from me. I let her go, sensing her sadness and confusion, and wondered what I had said wrong.

"What is it?" I asked.

"Do you want to be here? With me?" Marielle asked, a

frown on her face.

I frowned in response. "Of course I do, why would you ever think otherwise?"

"Because it sounds to me like you would leave if my guardian angel wanted you to, which suggests to me you're not really bothered either way. But because he, or she, or it, or whatever," Marielle's voice rose in frustration. "Thinks it's a good idea, that's okay, you'll stay."

I blinked. Women really were complicated creatures. I tried to gather my thoughts. "All I meant was, like your guardian angel, I want only the best for you. And if it was better for you that I leave, that's what I would do. Not because I wanted to leave you, but because I couldn't bear the idea of hurting you."

Marielle's frown dissolved, and she stepped back toward me. "If you don't want to hurt me, don't leave me again."

I nodded and wrapped my arms around her. "I won't."

Chapter Twelve

The next few days passed in a blur. Nathan stayed by my side the whole time, and together we sorted through the rest of the paperwork, clutter and rubbish. I made several trips to a local tip, and also to the village's one and only charity shop. Their initial excitement at the original donations soon turned into a look of dread whenever I set foot inside the shop bearing black bags.

After just two weeks, the tiny cottage resembled something of a home again. I hadn't removed all traces of my father. I had kept things I knew he had treasured, like the old photo albums and the family jewellery. The day I had found all the old photos was when the situation had finally hit me.

I was staring at a photo of me and my parents, taken a year before my mum had died, and the tears started. I hadn't allowed myself to properly grieve since arriving at the cottage, with everything that needed to be arranged and sorted, and in that moment, when everything was nearly finished, the reality of having no family left suddenly hit me.

I was alone.

And my boyfriend was a ghost.

Amidst the sobbing, even I had to laugh at that. I felt Nathan's energy before he spoke from the doorway of the bedroom.

"Are you okay?"

I shook my head, and the sobbing resumed. He came and sat on the floor, wrapping his arms around me, pulling me in close. He didn't try to stop my tears, or soothe my pain. He knew all I needed in that moment was to have him hold me.

After that episode, I had resumed as normal, but now all of the sorting and cleaning was done, and the paperwork was completed, I needed to make a decision.

What next?

It was around three in the afternoon, and I was doing the washing up in the now-clean kitchen, when there was a knock on the door. I dropped the bowl into the sink in surprise. I hadn't had any visitors at all the whole time I'd been there so far, and aside from Sarah, there was no one else who knew where I was.

I dried my hands and went to answer the door. Before I opened it, I turned around to see Nathan disappearing from his spot on the sofa. Though I knew he would be back as soon as I got rid of whoever was at the door, it still pained me to watch him go.

I turned the key and the door creaked open. I peered out into the late afternoon sunshine, to see the waitress from the café stood on the doorstep.

"Hi," I said, surprised.

She smiled and held out a box to me. "I thought you might like some more cake, seeing as you liked it so much when you came to the café the other day."

I blinked and took the box from her. "Wow, thanks, that's so nice of you, I don't know what to say." I peeked inside the box and saw two large slices of the gooey chocolate cake. Before I could think it through I opened the door wider. "Would you like to come in for a cuppa?"

Her smile widened and she nodded. "I'd love to."

She stepped inside, and I closed the door behind her, feeling very thankful she had not come any sooner and seen the terrible state the cottage was in previously. She followed me into the kitchen and I put the kettle on. I put the two slices of cake onto plates and offered her one.

"Oh, no thank you. If I eat any more cake I'll be the size of a house. Keep it for your boyfriend."

I set the plate on the counter. "I don't think you have much to worry about in that area." I frowned. "Boyfriend?"

"Yeah, Mrs Hammersmith down the road said you were living here with someone, I assumed it was your boyfriend, or is he your husband?"

I shook my head. So a lady down the road had seen Nathan. Interesting. I didn't know what to say. "Uh, no, it's just me here. It's my dad's house, he passed away a few weeks ago. Tea or coffee?"

"Oh my goodness, I'm so sorry, I didn't know, Mrs Hammersmith didn't mention that. I haven't lived in this area long, my husband and I moved here about three months ago. Um, coffee please."

I got the coffee out of the cupboard, and she continued.

"When I heard Mrs Hammersmith talking about you, and I realised you were the one who came in a couple of weeks back, I felt I should stop by. I know that when we moved in, no one made any attempt to welcome us, and I felt it would be nice to welcome you."

I smiled. "I'm glad you did." I made the coffee and handed her the mug. "And not just because you brought chocolate cake." I ate a small piece and closed my eyes. It really was delicious cake.

"Good?"

"Amazing," I said. "Would you like to come and sit down?"

She nodded and followed me through to the tiny lounge. I sat on the chair, and she sat on the sofa opposite me. The temperature seemed lower here, and I felt goose bumps raise on my arms. Nathan hadn't gone very far.

"So, can I ask what your name is?"

"Oh," she said, laughing. "I'm sorry. Must think I'm mad, getting myself invited in without even introducing myself. I'm Charlotte."

"Nice to meet you, Charlotte, I'm Marielle."

She smiled. "It's nice to meet you too. So, what do you do?"

I sighed. "I was in uni, until my dad died. I left the course to come and sort out the funeral and all his things here. We've only just finished sorting the house out." I winced a little when I realised I'd said we instead of I, but Charlotte didn't seem to notice.

"Yeah I think I saw you taking some bags to the charity shop once."

I laughed. "Yes, that was me. Made quite a few trips to the charity shop, I thought at one point they were going to ban me from bringing them any more stuff."

Charlotte giggled. "I'm sure they loved it really. At least it kept them busy."

I smiled. "It certainly did. So what brought you to this village?"

"My husband lost his job, so he started up an online business, which meant we no longer needed to be in the city. So we moved here, because he's always wanted to live in the countryside."

"The city?"

"Yes, we moved from London."

"Do you work with him? Or just at the café?" I laughed. "Sorry, I'm not trying to interrogate you, I'm just curious."

Charlotte smiled. "It's fair enough. No I don't work

with him, we'd kill each other if I did. I used to work in a coffee shop in London, but really, I want to be an actress."

I frowned. "I can't imagine there are many acting opportunities here?"

She sighed. "I know, there aren't any at all. I wasn't happy about moving at first. I couldn't see how I would make a go of my career stuck out here in the sticks. But I must admit, I do enjoy the peace and quiet." She smiled, but I could see the sadness in her eyes.

She didn't say anything else. She simply looked down at her mug of coffee.

"Don't let anyone take away your dreams, Charlie-Bear. Go after them. You only get one lifetime, live it to the full."

Charlotte's mug was broken on the old slate flooring before I realised that the words had come out of my own mouth.

"What?" she gasped.

*   *   *

I know I should have given her some warning, not just fed her the words straight from Charlotte's guardian angel, but it seems like a good idea in that moment. I take in Charlotte and Marielle's states of shock and think perhaps I was wrong.

"I don't know where that came from," Marielle sputters, oblivious to the puddle of coffee on the floor she's spent ages scrubbing clean.

"My grandmother used to say that to me," Charlotte whispers. "How did you know?"

Marielle shakes her head. "I don't know, I wasn't even really aware I was saying it." She sets her mug down on the coffee table and goes over to the sofa to sit next to Charlotte. She puts her arm around her. "I'm sorry, I really don't know what to say."

I look at Charlotte's guardian angel who is on the other side of Charlotte, also embracing her. Within a few moments, she seems calm again. She turns to look at Marielle. "Are you psychic? Or a medium?"

Marielle frowns. "I don't know, um, it's complicated."

"Tell her that Bluey is with her grandmother now," Charlotte's guardian angel says to me. I repeat the information to Marielle, and she says the words, without a second thought. Charlotte's eyes widen and she gasps.

"Are you talking to my grandmother right now?"

Marielle looks a little freaked out. It's funny really, considering she is essentially dating a ghost.

"No, I don't think so," she says. A look passes over her face and I see it dawn on her. She mouths my name.

"What is it?" Charlotte asks.

Marielle shakes her head. "It's kind of weird, and hard to explain."

"I don't have anywhere else I need to be right now."

Marielle smiles. "It's nothing really, there's just someone in spirit I have a connection to, and they talk to me. They must have just given me that information about your grandmother."

Though I can't feel hurt in this dimension, her words bother me. She dismisses our bond so easily, as though it means nothing to her, and I am just a random spook who haunts her.

"So can you ask him things?"

"Yes, I guess so. I've only done this once before, for my friend, but the answers were coming from the spirit I know, not from any relatives or other spirits."

"Well if you get any more messages, please let me know." Charlotte looks down at the broken mug and spillage, becoming aware of it suddenly. "I'm so sorry."

She jumps up. "I'll go get a towel or something."

Marielle watches her go to the kitchen. "There's some kitchen towel on the counter, and a dustpan and brush under the sink," she calls out. She seems unable to move from the sofa. I move closer to her, and whisper to her.

Are you okay?

Marielle closes her eyes and nods, reassuring me.

Charlotte returns and cleans up the mess, and Marielle seems to become aware of her surroundings again. "Thank you, Charlotte. You didn't have to do that, really."

"It's fine, I was the one who made the mess." She takes the broken china and wet paper towels back to the kitchen, and finds some newspaper to wrap up the sharp pieces before putting them in the bin.

Marielle gets up and follows her to the kitchen. "I'm sorry if I freaked you out."

Charlotte smiles. "It's okay, I think I needed to hear that. My gran was always right. And I know she used to worry I wouldn't follow my dreams, and I would just do whatever Jim wanted." She sighs. "And she was right. I didn't even really protest the move. I just wanted to do whatever made him happy." I can see her guardian angel trying to boost her energy, trying to envelop her in love, but I can also see a barrier of some kind around Charlotte, which is blocking the energy. I ask her guardian angel why that is.

"It happens when people stop listening to us, stop believing in us. The disbelief forms a layer of energy that blocks us out. I've been trying for a while to get that message through to her, but she just couldn't hear me. So thank you for doing that."

"You're welcome. Perhaps now if Marielle and Charlotte become friends, I can pass on more messages for you."

"Thank you."

I tune back into the conversation between the two women, Charlotte is at the front door, ready to leave. "Maybe I'll see you around sometime? We only live down the road. Just pop by if you need anything."

Marielle nods, and gives Charlotte a quick hug. "Thank you. I will."

"Bye."

Marielle closes the door and turns around, leaning heavily against it.

"Nathan, what the hell was that?"

*   *   *

"I don't think there is a hell."

I jumped when Nathan appeared right in front of me. He grinned, and some of my annoyance disappeared. "That really wasn't funny. Since when am I channelling messages from other dead people? I only just met the woman, she's going to think I'm a complete nutter now."

Nathan shook his head. "No, she won't. She needed that message, her angel had been trying to get it to her for ages."

I sighed. "Don't you think her angel could have waited until I at least knew her a little better?"

"I'm sorry. I will ask your permission next time."

"Please do. It freaked me out." I went to the kitchen to start making dinner. It was a bizarre thing, to be in a relationship with someone who didn't need feeding, who produced no mess, no washing, no washing up, and who didn't even need to have a shower or bath.

Perfect housemate, really.

I began to chop up onions, and Nathan took up his usual spot behind me at the tiny kitchen table.

"We should get a radio in here," Nathan commented.

"Why do you say that?" I asked. "Is my conversation too boring for you?"

Nathan chuckled. "No, of course not, it's just that perhaps if there was music in here you would dance around again."

I stopped chopping and turned to face Nathan, my cheeks burning. "You watched me dancing?"

He smiled. "Yes, and I remember wishing I could dance around with you."

I shook my head and turned away. "Maybe I'll look for one when I'm at the shops next."

"That would be good."

I decided to change the subject. "So what should I do? If Charlotte's angel knows what her dreams are and is urging her to follow them, what about me? What does my angel think I should be doing?"

There was silence while I finished chopping the onions and put them in a saucepan with some oil. I lit the gas ring and set the pan on top. I glanced over at Nathan, but he wasn't there.

Typical male. Ask a difficult question, and they disappear into another dimension rather than answer it.

The tomato and basil sauce was simmering and the pasta was nearly cooked by the time Nathan reappeared.

"Sorry, I can't speak to the angels when I'm in this dimension. I can't hear them."

"You just went to ask my angel my question?" I was surprised. I hadn't expected him to immediately go and find the answer.

"Yes. I asked your angel what you were meant to do."

"And what did he say?"

"That it will become clear in time."

I raised an eyebrow. I drained the pasta and put some

on my plate. I ladled the sauce on top and sprinkled some grated cheese. I sat down at the table opposite Nathan before speaking again. "Sounds to me like my angel doesn't really know."

Nathan sighed. "I know he does. I think it's the issue of free will. If they tell you what they think you should be doing, and you do it, but it doesn't work out the way you hoped, you would blame them. Because you didn't choose that path for yourself."

"But what if I make the wrong choice? Go down the wrong path? Wouldn't it be better for me to know where I'm meant to go?" I speared some penne with my fork and swirled it in the sauce, waiting for Nathan's thoughts.

He didn't disappear this time, but he was thoughtful for a few moments. "I don't think there is such a thing as the wrong path. There are many paths. Some them long, some short, some winding, some straight. But there is no wrong one."

I ate some more of my pasta while I thought about this. "Why does it matter what I do then? Why is my angel even bothering to guide me in any particular direction?"

Nathan smiled. "Because your angel wants you to live a life full of love, joy and happiness. But I think if he were to tell you how to follow that path, you wouldn't find it a fulfilling road. Sometimes, it's necessary to have a few obstacles along the way, it makes you stronger."

"Sounds like he just doesn't want to make it too easy for me."

Nathan laughed, and the sound of his amusement forced me to smile too. He reached across to hold my hand. His touch still gave me little shivers down my spine.

"You should listen to your intuition more, because more often than not, it is really the angels trying to keep you safe and guide you away from danger."

I tilted my head to the side. "Are you saying that the voices in my head really want the best for me?" I joked.

Nathan smiled. "Yes. They are trying to protect you."

A vague memory drifted through my mind. "Was it an angel who tried to stop me going to the fetish night?"

"No. That was me."

I sighed. "And I didn't listen. Do you know what happened that night? Because it's really just a huge blur to me."

"The guy who you were dancing with spiked the drink he bought you, and let's just say he did not have good intentions toward you."

My eyes widened. Though I had suspected I'd been drugged, it was a little bit scary to have it confirmed. "So what happened? Sarah said I left the Union with a guy, was it him?"

"No. It was me. It seems you could hear me more clearly while drugged. I guided you out of there and got you home." Nathan gripped my hand tightly. "I watched you all night to make sure you were okay."

Without warning, a tear slid down my cheek. "Thank you," I whispered. "I'm sorry I didn't listen, it could have turned out really bad." I frowned. "What happened to the guy?"

"Let's just say that in this case, the karma was pretty instant."

I smiled. "Good." I ate some more pasta, mentally thanking the angels again for blessing me with Nathan's presence in my life.

"So what have you decided?" Nathan asked.

I blinked, my fork paused mid-way to my mouth. "Decided?"

"About living here or selling up and moving."

I frowned. "I wasn't aware I'd made any decisions on

that front."

Nathan nodded, but looked unconvinced. I thought about it for a moment, and looked around the tiny little kitchen. I actually quite liked it here, now it was clean and tidy. The village was pretty quiet, not much seemed to happen, and aside from the odd nosy neighbour, it felt safe. I looked at Nathan. If we lived somewhere busier, our relationship couldn't continue. How could it?

Before I'd thought it through any further, I set my fork down and smiled at Nathan.

"I want to stay here. With you."

Nathan smiled back, but there was something in his eyes I couldn't read. He seemed both happy and sad about my decision.

"But you probably already knew I was going to say that, didn't you?"

*   *   *

Though time continued to have little meaning, I was pleased to spend the majority of it with Marielle, in her tiny cottage, living for the most part like a normal couple. We had a quiet Christmas, just the two of us. She bought herself a radio, and we enjoyed dancing in the kitchen.

Marielle was invited to spend Boxing Day with Charlotte and Jim. She didn't want to go without me, but I encouraged her to go. She needed to have some interaction with other people every now and then.

When the new year dawned, and the festivities were over, I noticed that Marielle seemed to get stressed out over the smallest things. Despite the frigid cold weather, she also went out quite often, usually under the pretence of picking up a pint of milk or some other kind of grocery. I never followed her, because I wanted her to feel like she had some alone time. Being together all the time just didn't seem fair somehow. But by the end of January, I couldn't ignore her behaviour any longer. Her stressed energy was putting me on edge.

I had thought about talking to her guardian angel about it, but that felt underhand somehow. If we were just a normal couple, I wouldn't have had that option anyway. And I didn't want to follow her, because that just felt wrong too.

I joined Marielle on the sofa one evening, and put my arm around her. She snuggled into my side.

"Are you going to tell me what's going on?" I asked, as gently as I could.

I felt her body stiffen up, and her breathing became shallow. "What do you mean?"

I squeezed her tightly. "You know what I mean. In the last few weeks you've been acting strangely, and you've been going out a lot, which is cool, but you seem to be even more stressed out when you return."

Marielle sighed, and her body softened against mine again. "I should have known I couldn't keep anything from you," she said. "I've been trying to find some work. The money in Dad's account is not going to last much longer, and if I don't find an income soon, I won't have any choice but to sell the house."

I felt stupid for not realising. I had assumed that what she had inherited would be enough for her to live on for longer than this, but I had never thought to ask. Mainly because I didn't have to worry about money, I didn't need anything. "Why didn't you say something? I could have been helping you to figure it out. Why did you feel the need to try and do it all by yourself?"

"It wasn't completely by myself, I've been chatting to Charlotte whenever I go out. I usually need the chocolate cake after traipsing from one place to the next, looking for a job."

"I still could have been helping you. What kind of jobs are you looking for?"

I felt Marielle shrugging. "It doesn't really matter, it could be anything, in a shop, café, office. I don't really mind."

I was quiet for a while. The idea of Marielle doing some mundane job just for the money seemed wrong somehow. I knew how intelligent and talented she was. She should definitely be making more than just the minimum wage. I also felt quite helpless and inadequate in that moment. If I were actually alive, I would be taking care of the money matters. It would be my responsibility to get the bills paid and food in the cupboards. I didn't care how antiquated the notion was, it was how it should have been.

But I couldn't do that. I held Marielle even more tightly. "Just let me know how I can help," I whispered.

"Okay."

*   *   *

"It's good to see you, Nathan."

"Good to see you too, angel," I reply. "I've become used to being in the human dimension. Though it's strange not to have the normal human needs."

"More convenient though, I should imagine."

"Absolutely. Now, you probably know why I've come to speak to you," I say to the angel. I know he's been watching everything, as he never leaves Marielle's side.

"Of course. Marielle is in need of work, and you want to help her, but don't know how."

"Yes. That's exactly it."

"There is a way you can help her."

"I'm listening."

"Her friend Charlotte is going to have an idea in the next couple of days. Marielle won't be convinced, but it is a good idea. And she will need your help to make it happen."

I am intrigued. "What kind of idea?"

"I'm afraid I cannot say. You will find out soon. But worry not, you will be able to take care of Marielle in the way you wish to."

So apparently my thoughts are seen by the angels too. Interesting.

"Thank you. I shall see you soon," I say.

"Yes, you will."

*　　　*　　　*

"You want me to do what?" I asked, not quite believing what Charlotte had just suggested.

"You don't like the idea? You said you needed to make some money soon."

I nodded. "I do, but I'm not a medium. Why on earth would people pay to have a reading from me?"

"Because medium or not, you are good. I mean," Charlotte settled into the chair across from me. "You gave me those messages from my grandmother. And you barely knew me, there's no way you could have known that."

I frowned. "But that could have been a one-off. What if I never get any more messages through?"

Charlotte smiled. "You could practice on me again if you like. Or you could do a reading one to one for the lady who suggested it. Her name is Donna. She will get to know how you work, and she'll be able to promote the event better."

"Event?" I echoed, feeling slightly queasy.

"Yeah, she knows pretty much everyone in the village, so I'm sure quite a few people would turn up to an evening of psychic mediumship with the magical Marielle."

I couldn't help but grin at the silly title she had come up with. The idea of me being magical seemed a little ridiculous. But I was also in a serious relationship with a spirit. So I wasn't exactly normal.

"Tell you what, invite Donna round to my house tomorrow night, around seven? And please come as well, just in case it all goes horribly wrong and I need a friend after."

Charlotte laughed and stood up. She patted me on the shoulder. "I'll see you tomorrow at seven." She went back to work and I finished my latte and chocolate cake. I thought about Charlotte's crazy idea. Charging a bunch of people to hear me relate messages from the other side? The idea just seemed so mad I couldn't get my head around it. It wasn't quite the nine-to-five retail assistant position I had been searching for. I would have to talk to Nathan about it, after all, I couldn't do it without him; he was my only link to the other world.

I left the café, and made my way back to my car. Ten minutes later, I was back at the cottage. As soon as I stepped through the door, my nose stopped me. Was that pizza I could smell?

"Welcome home." A floury, tomato-stained Nathan came out to the hallway to greet me.

I raised an eyebrow. "You cooked?" This was a first.

Nathan shrugged. "I realised that though I may not need to eat, or do the normal human stuff, I could at least help you out more, especially if you're going to be getting a job very soon."

I smiled. "Yeah, about the job thing, there's something I need to talk to you about."

"Tell me about it over dinner, it's pretty much done."

I set my handbag down in the hall and followed Nathan into the kitchen. It looked like he had used every pan and utensil in the kitchen. I said nothing as he ushered me to the dining table. It was set beautifully, with a tablecloth, candle, and he'd even picked out matching cutlery. I was surprised and incredibly touched.

Nathan placed my dinner in front of me with a flourish, and I had to admit, though it looked very much like homemade pizza, it smelled better than any pizza I'd ever had before.

Nathan sat in his usual spot, looking exhausted, but pleased with himself. I dug into the pizza, despite the fact I'd just eaten a large piece of chocolate cake.

"Good?" Nathan asked. I nodded, my mouth full. He let me eat for a few minutes, then asked, "So what did you need to talk to me about?"

Chapter Thirteen

The following night, I watch from the angel dimension as Marielle opens the door to her guests, and after introductions, they move to the lounge. Donna is chatting about her favourite mediums and how she loves to get readings. Marielle is looking even more nervous now than she was earlier, and I see her hand is shaking as she pours the tea. I look up at her guardian angel, who is doing his best to soothe her with his calming energy.

I look over to the two women, and I realise I can now see their angels too. They greet me, and tell me they will pass on any information that seems appropriate.

"Thank you," I reply, turning my attention back to the conversation in the room.

"So how does it work?" Donna is asking. "Do you need to know anything? Do you need something to hold, or do you use cards?"

"Um, no, I don't need anything. I'll just, um, see if anything comes through." The women fall silent for a moment, and I look up at Donna's guardian angel.

"Her mother, Jane, is in spirit. She passed away two years ago. She was joined by her husband, Donna's dad, a few months later. They are together, in spirit."

I relay the information to Marielle and she says it out loud. Donna's smile drops and she looks shocked.

"Her mother collected a particular type of china, from

a place in Wales, called Portmerion. Her father always hated it, he said it was too flowery for him."

Donna's look of shock deepens. I get the feeling she has never had such detailed information in a reading before.

"Just after they both passed, Donna got upset, and smashed several of the plates. Her mother wants her to know that it's okay, it doesn't matter that they were broken, she understands she was grieving."

Donna has come out of her state of shock, and starts to cry. Charlotte puts her arm around her, and the sound of her sobbing brings Marielle out of the slight trance she has gone into, in her effort to hear me clearly.

"Are you okay?" Marielle asks her. "I'm sorry, I really have no idea what will come through. I'm very new at this. I don't know how to control it."

Donna shakes her head. "No, it's okay, really." She pulls out a hankie and wipes her tears. "It's amazing, I've never had such detailed information so quickly before," she says, confirming my thoughts. "I was really upset after I broke the plates. My mum had collected them for years and I didn't think she'd forgive me for doing that."

Marielle smiles, looking relieved. "Should I continue?"

Donna nods. "Please."

"Donna has a sister, but they haven't spoken since their parents died, because of a dispute about the will."

The evening wears on and turns into night. The information flows from Donna's angel, to me, to Marielle, and then to Donna. After several hours, Marielle is looking exhausted, and Donna seems totally overwhelmed. I stop the angel mid-sentence. "I think it's time to call it a night," I say to her. She agrees.

"Just one last thing though? Tell Donna that the touch she feels on her forehead at night is her mother kissing her and whispering: 'Goodnight, Poppet'."

I tell Marielle that, and also tell her the reading is over.

Marielle gives Donna the last message, and her eyes well up again. She doesn't bother to wipe away her tears.

"Thank you, thank you so much, Marielle," Donna says, leaning across the coffee table to take Marielle's hands. She squeezes them in her own. "You have no idea how much I needed to hear everything you said tonight. You have a gift." She lets go and stands up. "I would love to book you for an event. We'll start small, I'll put the feelers out and scope a couple of venues. How does that sound?"

Marielle is too exhausted to do anything other than nod.

"Excellent. Thank you again." Donna looks at Charlotte, who is also nearly asleep. "Are you ready to go, Charlotte? I think Marielle needs to get some rest."

I watch the two ladies leave. Marielle just about manages to get up to see them to the door. She can barely utter the words to say goodbye. I am a little worried about her.

She goes back into the lounge and slumps down onto the chair. I leave the angel dimension and am immediately by her side.

*   *   *

"Are you okay?"

She nodded her head once. "Just so sleepy," she whispered. She closed her eyes and her head fell to the side. Without thinking about it, I put my arms around her and lifted her up. She rested her head on my shoulder and I carried her up the tiny, narrow stairs to the bedroom. I laid her on the bed and pulled the covers over her, before going back downstairs to lock up and turn off the lights. When I joined her in bed, she was snoring softly.

"I love you," I whispered into her ear. I was surprised when she smiled in her sleep.

* * *

As my dream slipped away, I awoke feeling completely disorientated. I blinked and rubbed my eyes, then sat up. I was fully clothed, in bed, by myself. The bedroom door opened and Nathan appeared, holding a tray with breakfast on it.

He smiled at me and I smiled back. I liked this new, helpful version of him, it certainly made me feel a little less alone in getting things done. He set the tray down on the bed and put his hand on mine.

"How are you feeling this morning?"

I frowned at the serious tone of his voice. "I'm fine," I said, noticing that my throat felt a bit scratchy. I remembered the events of the previous evening. I searched my memory, but I couldn't remember Donna and Charlotte leaving or coming upstairs and getting into bed.

"What happened? After the reading?"

Nathan smiled and handed me a glass of orange juice. "You were pretty out of it, I carried you up to bed after Donna and Charlotte left."

I drank the juice and smiled. "Thank you. I guess being a medium is actually pretty tiring."

"It would seem so. You'll have to be careful not to overdo it when you do the events."

I groaned. As well as the reading had gone, the idea of doing readings for a roomful of strangers filled me with so much dread. What if Nathan wasn't able to get any messages? What if I looked like a total fraud and fool?

Nathan patted my hand. "Don't worry about it. I will make sure it all goes smoothly. I won't let you look foolish."

I raised an eyebrow. "Is our bond so strong now that you can read my every thought?"

Nathan chuckled. "No, I just figured that was what you were thinking, based on your groan."

"We really have been spending way too much time together."

"Definitely."

I punched Nathan lightly in the side. "You say that like it's a bad thing."

"It's not, I was just teasing."

"You better be," I said, teasing him back. I picked up a piece of buttery toast and bit into it, suddenly feeling ravenous. "So you promise not leave me in front of a roomful of strangers with nothing to say?"

"I promise."

I stuffed down the second slice of toast. "Good."

*   *   *

Later in the day, I kissed Nathan goodbye and popped into the village to see Charlotte. Even though I was no longer looking for work, I had got used to our afternoon chats over tea and chocolate cake, and I wanted to find out what she had thought of the previous evening.

As soon as I pulled into the car park, I saw the poster.

"An Evening with Mystical Marielle," I read from the brightly coloured paper, attached to the lamppost next to the car park ticket machine.

"Are you getting a ticket, or not?" a man asked impatiently. I hadn't even noticed him standing behind me. I waved him forward, and he got his ticket. I was transfixed by the brightly coloured poster. Apparently, I would be performing next Saturday, and the tickets were a bargain at twenty quid per person.

I could feel the blood draining from my face, and I wondered how on earth Donna had managed to arrange an event so quickly. And who the hell would pay twenty quid just to spend the evening with me?

Eventually, I pulled myself out of my trance and got my ticket. After putting it on the inside of the windscreen, I set off to the café. The posters were EVERYWHERE. Every lamppost, every shop window, even tucked under the windscreen wipers of parked cars.

I felt a little annoyed that Donna hadn't actually asked me if I was able to do Saturday. But who was I kidding? It wasn't like I had a packed schedule, and Donna knew that.

I reached the café and as soon as I stepped inside, I knew that my safe haven had been breached too. There was a flyer on every table. I caught Charlotte's eye as I settled down at my usual table, and she gave me an apologetic glance.

When she had finished serving a customer, she came over to me. "I'm so, so sorry," she said in a hushed voice. "I had no idea she would work this quickly to arrange an event. I think you blew her away last night."

"Does she honestly think people will pay twenty quid to come and see me? It seems a bit extortionate, don't you think?"

"Not really, it's cheaper than a night out on the town, but way better for the soul." Charlotte grinned and I sighed.

"I guess," I said, knowing my voice lacked any enthusiasm.

Charlotte patted my shoulder. "It will all be great. Would you like the usual?"

I nodded and she whirled away to get my latte and chocolate cake. I played with the salt and pepper shakers while I waited, and tried to convince myself it all would work out alright. A cold gust of wind made me look up, and there in the doorway, was Donna.

She made a beeline for me, a huge smile on her face. Without waiting to be invited, she sat down opposite me. "Good morning! I hope you got enough sleep last night, you looked exhausted when we left."

I blinked. "Um, yeah, I slept like the dead."

Donna looked a little shocked, then she started laughing. "Like the dead, now that is funny." Charlotte arrived with my order.

"Hey, Donna, can I get you anything?"

"Yes please, Charlotte. I'll have a cappuccino and a flapjack please."

She nodded and went back to the kitchen. I ate a forkful of cake and waited for Donna to speak. I could see she was bursting to tell me something.

Sure enough, a few seconds later, Donna leaned across the table toward me. "I've already sold twenty advance tickets," she stage-whispered.

I dropped the fork onto the plate. "S-s-s-eriously?" I stuttered. "How big is the venue?"

"It can hold up to a hundred, so I plan on selling a lot more tickets, but it's a good start, don't you think?"

I knew my eyes were wide and my mouth had dropped open, but I couldn't rearrange my expression.

After a few seconds, Donna lost her look of excitement and peered at me in concern. "Are you okay?"

I closed my mouth and blinked a few times. Finally, I nodded. "Uh huh, yeah, I'm fine, just a little surprised."

Donna smiled again, and Charlotte arrived at our table with her order. I picked up the fork again, and absentmindedly ate more cake. We ate and drank in silence for a while, my mind was a chaotic whir. There might be a hundred people on Saturday. A hundred. Considering I had only done one proper reading, and that was to one person, the idea of having so many faces there, staring at me, freaked me out completely. But another part of my mind was working out the financial side. A hundred people paying twenty pounds each was two grand. For one night. I'd never even made that much in a month before.

As if she were reading my mind, Donna broke the silence. "I probably should have said about how the event will work. I figured that once the hire of the village hall is covered, which is fifty pounds, and the cost of the advertising is taken out, you should have a nice amount of cash for the night."

I frowned. "What about you? You will be taking a percentage, won't you?"

Donna shook her head. "No, this is just what I do. I don't do it for the money. I'm always organising local events."

I shook my head in response. "Well this time you will be getting paid. Because the only reason there will be people there is because of you. So I insist you take a percentage of the profits."

Donna smiled. "Thank you, I appreciate that."

"Thank *you*," I said, returning the smile. "I really do appreciate all you are doing for me, and if I seem a little weird, it's just nerves kicking in. I've never been keen on public speaking, and doing readings in front of a hundred people just seems like a scary concept."

"I understand, I used to be as shy as a dormouse. Now I run a whole bunch of local groups, and often talk at the local parish council meetings."

"How did you get over being shy?" I asked.

"You'll think I'm crazy if I tell you what I did."

I raised my eyebrows and swallowed some cake. "Um,

it can't be that odd, surely?"

Donna laughed. "I guess considering you talk to dead people, it probably won't seem odd at all. I used EFT to get rid of my fear of public speaking."

My face must have looked completely blank, because Donna launched into an explanation of what EFT was.

"It stands for Emotional Freedom Technique. You tap different points on your body," she said, demonstrating on her own hand and face. "And while you tap, you say things like 'Even though I'm terrified of public speaking, I totally love and accept myself'. Or 'Even though I'm afraid of looking stupid in front of a hundred people, I totally love and accept myself'. Once you've been through the sequence with the negative, you do it again with the positives. So things like 'I am confident, and I speak to large groups with ease'. Or 'I enjoy public speaking, and I enjoy helping lots of people at once'."

My face must have now had a look of total disbelief on it, because Donna continued, this time sounding a little defensive.

"It works, honestly. Ever since I did the tapping initially, I've never felt nervous while speaking in front of large crowds. And the weird thing is, I now actually really enjoy myself when I do it."

I nodded and sipped my latte. "Okay, I believe you. It just seems so bizarre."

"I'm pretty sure they have a couple of books about it in the bookshop two doors down. You should go check them out." Donna slurped down the rest of her cappuccino and quickly chewed the last two bites of her flapjack. "I better get going," she said, pushing her chair back and standing up. "These tickets aren't going to sell themselves."

I watched her go and settle her bill, then leave the café. Despite her reassurances, I couldn't help but wonder what the hell I had got myself into.

*   *   *

I was just checking on the lasagne in the oven when I heard the front door of the cottage open and close. I closed the oven door and turned to see Marielle standing in the kitchen doorway.

"Hey, you," I said. "Have you had a good day? Dinner won't be long."

She nodded. "It smells good, thank you for cooking again."

I shrugged. "I'm actually starting to enjoy it." I took the oven mitts off and put them down, crossing the tiny room in two steps to join her in the doorway. Her energy felt muddled and confused. "What's wrong?"

She shook her head. "Nothing, it's just been a bit of a weird day. Donna has arranged a psychic night for Saturday, with me as the main attraction."

"Wow, that's really quick. She was impressed last night, obviously."

"It would seem so. I'm just nervous, that's all." She held up a paper shopping bag, bearing the logo of an open book. "I went to the bookshop and got a book Donna recommended for getting rid of my fears of public speaking."

I took the book out of the bag and read the title. "I'm sure it'll be useful, though I've never heard of the technique before. But is there any need to be nervous? It won't be that big a group. This village is pretty small. And I'm sure the percentage of people who believe in psychics is even smaller."

"The hall will hold a hundred people, and Donna has sold twenty tickets already. She's plastered the village with posters and flyers too."

I could tell that Marielle was getting more agitated talking about it, so I put the book back in the bag. "Why don't you go and relax in the lounge for a bit, I'll bring you some wine. Then you can have dinner and we can chill out for the evening?"

Marielle shook her head and picked up the bag. "No, I need to read this as soon as possible, I want to be prepared."

I smiled. "I'll call you when it's ready." I kissed her on the forehead and she retreated into the lounge. When I took the glass of wine to her a few minutes later, she was holding the book in one hand, and was tapping her index finger on her cheekbone with the other.

I put the glass on the coffee table and left her to it, not wanting to disturb the process. I knew the event on Saturday would be fine, no matter how many people turned up. But I didn't think my reassurances would make her feel any better. After all, I had nothing to lose, whereas if it all went wrong, she would be the one who would get a bad reputation or be blamed for it.

I made a salad and set it out on her plate, trying to be as artistic as possible. I laid the table, and placed the steaming lasagne in the middle.

Marielle was distracted throughout the meal, though she seemed to enjoy my cooking again. I was quiet too, because I didn't know what to say to make the situation easier. I decided I should go to the angel dimension tonight, while Marielle slept, to talk to her guardian angel. Perhaps he would know how to reassure Marielle.

It was midnight before Marielle finally relinquished her book and went to bed. It seemed that the weird tapping thing was having a positive effect on her, as she seemed a little more relaxed. I waited for a few minutes, until her breathing was slow and even in the darkness, then I slipped out of the human realm.

*   *   *

"Nathan."

"Hello, angel. You probably know why I'm here," I say.

"Yes, and don't worry, it's all working out as planned. It seems at least Donna has no trouble listening to her guardian angel."

I laugh. "So what is the bigger purpose to Marielle doing these readings? It's obviously more than just providing her with an income."

"Of course. The reason is for important messages to be delivered from the guardian angels to their charges. There are many mediums and psychics all around the world who do this very important work, but few have such clear and direct contact as Marielle. For many, the messages are being delivered in metaphorical, distorted, visual or patchy ways. Your connection with Marielle is so clear and so strong that she is relaying the messages word for word."

"I understand. Though I must admit, I still don't quite understand why our bond is so strong, so deep. Why couldn't we have just got together when I was still alive? Our relationship is amazing but I can't help being sad at the fact that it's just not real."

The angel looks down at Marielle's sleeping face, lit up by the full moon peering through the thin curtains. "What do you mean it's not real?" he asks softly.

Despite the feeling of peace that pervades this dimension, I can't help but feel a glimmer of frustration and impatience. "We can't go out in public together, we can't get married, we can't have children, or grandchildren and Marielle will basically be single for the entire relationship, in the eyes of others. So it's not real. If it were, we'd be able to do those things."

The angel looks up at me, his gaze piercing right through my soul. "What if I told you that if you had got together and had a relationship when you were still living, it might well have been the same story?"

"What do you mean?"

"I mean, you might not have got married, and you might not have been able to have children. Therefore you wouldn't have had grandchildren."

I don't know what to say. It hasn't occurred to me that we could in fact be living the exact same reality as we would have, had our relationship occurred before I died. My guilt disappears. But in its place, a new concern appears.

"But someone else could still give her those things. Couldn't they?"

"It's possible."

I am silent for a while, and I watch Marielle turn over in bed, her hand reaching out for me in her sleep. She seems agitated when her hand hits the empty side of the bed, but she doesn't wake up. A few minutes later, she settles down again.

"Will you tell me when it's time for me to leave and let her have all of those things that I cannot give her?"

This time, it is the angel who is silent for a while.

"Yes, I will."

*　　　*　　　*

Saturday arrived far too quickly. Even though Sarah had come to show her support, and I had done an extensive amount of tapping and various other things, I still felt nervous as I waited to be introduced to the audience. Nathan and I had been practicing the routine, and I knew it would go fine, but I think what worried me most was my inability to censor anything that came through. The messages would come out of my mouth before I even had a chance to process them, what if I said something that hurt or upset someone?

I felt a wave of calm wash over me and I smiled as I recognised the energy. Nathan was doing his best to reassure me from where he was in the angel dimension.

I heard Donna announce my name, and I took a deep breath and entered the room through the side door. Donna had wanted me to do the readings from the stage, but the idea didn't sit well with me. I wanted to be at the same level as everyone else in the room, not above and separate from them.

There was a round of applause as I entered, and I was amazed that a roomful of people (and yes, as I feared, the room was completely full) were clapping for me when they didn't know who I was, and before this week they would never have heard of me before. Donna really was a miracle worker.

I reached my chair and held up a hand, the clapping ceased immediately and my eyes widened a little. I wasn't used to having so many people respond to me like that, and it made me feel a little panicky again.

I'm here, Nathan said, calming me. *We are ready whenever you are.*

I sat down and closed my eyes briefly, while I calmed and centred myself, using one of the techniques I'd read about earlier in the week. Knowing I couldn't delay any further, I opened my eyes and stood up. My gaze rested on Sarah, who was sat in the front row. She winked at me and smiled, making me feel at ease.

"I'm getting a message for the lady in the fourth row, wearing the green top with the flower embroidery on it."

Even though I couldn't see her and her clothing in front of me, these details flowed through me.

A lady in the fourth row stood up. "That's me."

I nodded. "Your mother passed away just two months ago, and you had been caring for her for the previous five years."

She nodded, but I wasn't really looking for, or waiting for confirmation of the information, I was just pausing to relax further and let the words flow.

"She wants you to know she appreciates everything you did for her, and she knows you have been feeling angry and frustrated at your siblings who have been coming out of the woodwork to claim her things and her money."

The woman nodded again, and I was vaguely aware she had tears rolling down her cheeks.

"She wants you to know that none of it matters. That everyone will get what is rightly theirs, and no amount of stuff could ever be as important as the bond the two of you shared. She also wants to make sure you keep the china Humpty Dumpty."

I paused, only because my brain caught up with my words and what I had just said sounded utterly ridiculous. There was a wave of giggles around the room, but when I looked at the woman, she had her hand over her mouth and seemed to be in shock.

"How did you know?" she whispered.

I ignored her question and continued. "Keep it safe, and when everything has been sorted, and the dust settles, you need to re-enact the nursery rhyme in which Humpty Dumpty is the star." Again, the absurdity of my words made me pause, and I even felt the need to talk to Nathan for a moment.

Nathan, what the hell is this about? I asked him silently.

Don't worry, it will make sense to her soon enough. Just keep going, you're doing great.

I looked at the woman who was also looking confused. "You want me to smash him?"

"Your mum wants you to play out the nursery rhyme, but not, and I will repeat, NOT until all of the legal stuff is finalised and everything is settled."

The lady nodded. I knew I was finished with her message, so I gestured for her to sit down again.

"There's a man in the sixth row, wearing a pink t-shirt, and has a tattoo of a ladybird on his arm," I said, moving onto the next message without much of a pause.

A man stood up, a look of astonishment on his face. "That's me."

I nodded and launched into his message. All trace of my nerves had gone, and I relaxed into the flow.

*   *   *

"I think we ought to stop there for the night, everyone," I announce to the many guardian angels present. They all nod in agreement. Though we never tire, here in the angelic dimension, we can all see that Marielle is now exhausted. I glance up at the clock, she has been relaying messages for nearly four hours.

Marielle, I say. *There are no more messages for tonight. Just tell everyone here that their guardian angels are present with them at all times, and all they need to do is ask for their help, guidance and protection, and they will be more than happy to help.*

Marielle repeats my words to the room, and thanks everyone for coming. She receives another round of applause, then people begin to rise from their seats, stretching their limbs and shaking themselves awake. Despite the late hour and her obvious exhaustion, a line forms and Marielle is inundated with words of thanks and hugs and handshakes.

It seems she is a hit.

It's an hour later before Marielle is finally able to make it out the door, with a rather large amount of cash in her pocket. Sarah is waiting for her at the door, and together they make their way to Marielle's car. Much like I did the night of the fetish ball, I stay close to Marielle's side, keeping both her and Sarah safe as they cross the car park. I keep up a stream of random conversation in Marielle's head to keep her awake on the short drive home, as Sarah seems to be quiet too.

Once they reach the cottage and are safely inside, I watch as Marielle makes them both a hot chocolate, and the two women settle on the sofa. Marielle seems to be operating on autopilot, and I know she will crash very soon.

"You were amazing tonight," Sarah says softly. "How did you do it? I mean, just a few months ago you weren't able to do that. Have you been training with someone?"

Marielle shakes her head. "No. It's just my connection with Nathan. I talk to him, he talks to the guardian angels of other people, and they give him information to pass to me." Marielle shrugged. "I didn't even know it was possible until a few weeks ago."

"That's amazing. Has your connection with him become clearer?"

Marielle nearly chokes on her hot chocolate as she laughs. "Yes, it's very clear now."

I know she isn't telling Sarah the full story because she doesn't think she will believe her, or understand. But I feel a glimmer of sadness that Marielle is being forced to live a lie. She can't tell anyone she is in a relationship with a ghost.

Marielle finishes her drink and struggles to her feet. "I

think I need to get to bed, I'm just shattered."

Sarah nods. "Of course. It's been a long night."

Marielle touches her arm. "I'm sorry you didn't get any messages tonight."

"Don't be silly, there was no one I needed to hear from. Did you ever hear from your mum, or your dad?"

Marielle smiles. "Yes, they're together now on the other side. He apologised to my mum for not believing in her." Marielle wipes away a tear and Sarah smiles up at her.

"That's awesome."

"Yeah," Marielle agrees. "I've made up the bed in the small bedroom. It's the door on the left at the top of the stairs."

"Thank you. I'll be off to bed soon too."

Marielle nods and is overcome with a massive yawn. "I'll see you in the morning," she tells Sarah, before slowly making her way up the stairs.

*   *   *

Once Marielle closed the bedroom door, I re-joined the human dimension and helped her to change into her pyjamas. I got into bed beside her, warming the chilly sheets with our combined heat.

"You really were quite incredible tonight," I whispered into her ear.

She smiled. "I couldn't have done it without you."

Within seconds, her breathing deepened and she was fast asleep.

I kissed her cheek and closed my eyes.

Chapter Fourteen

I felt disorientated when I awoke on Sunday morning. Usually my nights were filled with vivid dreams, but it seemed the evening of channelling had exhausted me enough to put me into a deeper sleep. Because I couldn't remember dreaming at all.

"Good morning."

Nathan's deep voice whispering in my ear gave me the shivers. I turned to face him, and he leaned down to kiss me softly on the lips.

"Good morning," I replied when he pulled away.

"You're so beautiful," he murmured, making me smile.

I ran my hand through my bird's nest hair and laughed. "I think you need to go to Specsavers."

Nathan shook his head, not even cracking a smile. "I mean it. You are beautiful." He stroked my cheek with his thumb. "I love you."

Though I had a vague memory of him saying these three words to me before, it was still a surprise to me. Without even needing to think about it, I replied, "I love you, too." I reached up to touch his face, and it struck me once again what a miracle it was to have him in my life. I still had no idea how it was possible, but I was so very grateful it was happening.

Half an hour later, I dragged myself away from Nathan, and got out of bed.

I got washed and dressed, before heading downstairs. I looked into the lounge, and saw that Sarah was up and dressed already. She seemed to be absorbed in reading my book on mediumship.

"Morning," I said, making her jump.

"Goodness," she gasped. She took a moment to compose herself. "Morning."

I chuckled. "Sorry, didn't meant to startle you."

She smiled. "It's okay, it's just because I was reading about contacting the dead, that's all." She stood up and stretched, putting the book down on the coffee table. She followed me into the kitchen.

"Have you had anything to eat yet?" I asked her, filling the kettle.

"No, I thought I would wait for you."

"Do you fancy pancakes?" I asked.

Sarah settled herself into Nathan's usual chair at the dining table. "Yes, please." After a few moments of shifting about, trying to get comfortable, she gave up and switched to my usual seat, where she settled immediately. I smiled to myself and set about making the pancake mixture.

"You can keep the book if you're enjoying it," I said. I knew I wouldn't ever need it again.

"Are you sure?"

"Of course." I cracked the egg into the bowl and whisked the egg, flour and milk together. I put the frying pan on the stove and got the oil nice and hot before pouring the mixture into it.

Fifteen minutes later, we were both tucking into our pancakes that were smothered in Nutella with sliced bananas on top. I sat in Nathan's chair, which felt really strange. I wondered where he was, whether he was still upstairs in his human body, or if he was chilling out with the angels. Though I was happy Sarah was here, I missed not being able to have Nathan here too.

"So what's next?" Sarah asked between mouthfuls.

"What do you mean?"

"Are you going to do more events? Are you going to do some events outside of this village too?"

I shrugged. "To be honest, I just haven't thought about it. I guess I could see what Donna thinks. She's the lady who organised last night. Considering how quickly she got the whole thing together she's probably booked a whole load more by now."

"At least you don't have to worry about that side of things. It's nice she has taken it upon herself to do that."

"Yeah, though I made sure she got paid for her time and effort. She didn't want anything from it to begin with, but I don't see why she shouldn't benefit from it." I sighed. "I have to admit though, at first I really hated the idea of charging people for readings."

"Why? They're paying for your time and energy, what's wrong with that?"

"It just didn't feel right. After all, it's not like I've been studying for years, or have any qualifications in this area at all. It's really just pure fluke that I'm suddenly able to get these messages, and it could all stop at any time."

Sarah finished her pancakes. "Better make the most of it while you can." She smiled. "So what are we doing today?"

"I thought we could go for a nice long walk and end up at the café. You can meet Charlotte. She wasn't there last night because it was her husband's birthday."

"Sounds good to me."

I stood up and took our dishes to the sink. "I really haven't had the chance to explore the local walks yet, it would be nice to be able to do that with someone."

"Let's do it." Sarah stood up too and headed upstairs to get ready. I rinsed the plates and cups and put them on the side to wash later. I went to find some thick socks to wear, and found that the bedroom was empty, which answered my earlier wondering.

I grabbed some socks out of the drawer and headed back downstairs to where Sarah was waiting for me. Once we had togged up, we set off out the door, and headed for the nearby woods.

*   *   *

I remained absent for the rest of Sarah's visit, only slipping into bed late each night to be with Marielle. I spent my time checking in on some old friends and my family. I was pleased to see they seemed to be okay, and they were moving on without me. I left a few little signs to show I had visited, as I wanted to give them a little comfort.

I spoke to their guardian angels, who filled me in on all that had transpired after my departure. They were doing a good job of keeping them safe for me, which I appreciated.

Sure enough, just two weeks after the first one, Donna arranged another event for Marielle, and yet again filled the hall to capacity. Marielle was more relaxed this time round, and the messages flowed even more quickly before. I was impressed with the way she kept up with the steady stream of information. The scene was the same afterward – everyone who had received a reading lined up to hug her, thank her and shake her hand. She was quickly becoming something of a local celebrity, which I teased her about afterward.

"Oh, don't be silly, Nathan," she said to me, the next morning. "It's just because this is such a small place. I'm not famous, not at all."

"If Donna has her way, you will be soon," I said, grinning at her while she sat across from me, eating her breakfast.

Marielle shook her head. "I'm happy to just do these local events. World-wide fame doesn't appeal to me at all."

I frowned. "Why not?"

Marielle swallowed a mouthful of cereal. "Isn't it obvious? How could we possibly have a relationship if there were paparazzi outside the windows taking photos of me? I would look like a crazy lady who was talking to herself. Take right now, for instance," she said, gesturing to the window and then to me. "The windows are only single-glazed. To anyone looking in or listening it would essentially look like I'm talking to an empty chair right now."

I looked at the window with its thin net covering, then back to Marielle. I tried to picture the scene the way someone looking in would see it, and I had to admit it would look odd.

The subject of being famous didn't come up for the rest of the day, we just relaxed and listened to music, and played some card games. But all day, what she had said played heavily on my mind. What else was she giving up to be with me?

She was already giving up on marriage, having children, even just having a meal out with her partner, because I couldn't do that for her. Now she was giving up being very successful out of fear she wouldn't be able to be with me.

"Nathan?"

I looked up at Marielle, who was waving her hand in front of my eyes. I wondered how long she had been trying to get my attention.

"Where were you just now?" she asked softly. "You certainly weren't in this dimension."

I smiled. "I'm sorry, I was lost inside my thoughts."

"What were you thinking?" she asked, putting the cards away.

I sighed. "I was thinking about everything you were giving up, to be with me."

Marielle went still for a moment, then she put the pack of cards down and came over to sit next to me. "You're not thinking of disappearing on me again are you?"

I took her hand and squeezed it gently. "No, I'm not. It just bothers me, that's all. I'm never going to be able to give you all the things you want. All the things you deserve. It just feels so selfish of me." I smoothed her hair away from her face and drank in her silvery grey eyes. "I don't want you to miss out on all the things I never got to experience."

Marielle's breath caught, and I could see she had never seen it from that perspective before. She was silent for a while, and I waited for her to speak again.

"It's not that I don't want to experience those things," Marielle whispered. She looked up at me, and I could see tears filling her eyes. "But I feel like we are meant to be together, we are meant to have this time, and I'm really not ready for it to end. When I'm with you, I don't feel like I'm missing out on anything. I feel like I have come home."

I wiped one of her tears away with my thumb. "I don't want to upset you. But I don't know how long this can continue. I mean, I assume at some point I will need to move on, and so will you."

Her tears were falling freely now, and Marielle made no move to wipe them away. "Okay," she whispered. "But until then, can we just pretend we will be together forever?"

I tried to smile, but my heart was breaking. "Of course," I said, pulling her into my arms and holding her tightly.

"Forever."

*   *   *

As well as the steady stream of events Donna organised for me, locally and in neighbouring towns and villages, I began to get requests for one to one readings. Soon I was spending every evening with a stranger sat across from me, and Nathan inside my mind. I missed our lazy evenings together, playing games and talking. Spring turned into summer, which slipped by too quickly into autumn.

One evening, I was getting ready for another client to arrive. I had eaten early and was just cleaning up the kitchen when I heard a knock at the front door.

I opened the door and found a man standing there. I recognised him from some of the events in the village hall.

Hi," I said, stepping aside and waving him in.

"Hello," he replied, stepping inside the house, ducking a little under the low doorway. "I'm–"

"Jack. Yes, it's nice to meet you." I took his jacket and offered him a drink. Soon, we were in the lounge, sat opposite each other. He looked quite comfortable on the sofa, like he was in his own home.

"This is a beautiful cottage," he commented, looking around.

"Thank you, it was my dad's. I inherited it last autumn."

"I see, sorry to hear that. Were you close?"

I shook my head. "No, in fact we hadn't spoken for quite some time before he passed."

Jack frowned. "Oh. That must have been difficult. Is that when you started speaking to spirit?"

I shook my head. "Actually, it was just before then, but not much before. My dad passing away wasn't really what started all of this."

"What was?"

Without intending to, I started telling him about Nathan. But I didn't mention that he actually became human. I made it sound like I could hear, feel and see Nathan, but in a sense of him being a spirit.

Jack was enthralled by my story, and kept asking more questions.

"See that's the thing with these readings I do," I said. "I don't actually speak to any of the deceased relatives, the only one I can speak to is Nathan. He talks to the guardian angels of my clients, and the angels tell him everything he needs to relay to me."

"That is just fascinating, I don't think I've ever heard of that kind of mediumship before."

I shrugged. "Me neither. It's just how it seems to work for me." I felt a mental nudge and recognised Nathan's energy. I smiled. "Speaking of which, I'm getting a nudge to begin your reading. I don't want to use up all your time talking about myself."

"Not at all, I have enjoyed talking to you. But please, do begin."

I took a deep breath and relaxed, allowing Nathan's words to flow through me to Jack.

*   *   *

"He fancied you."

I paused in the act of switching off my bedside lamp and turned to face Nathan. "Excuse me?"

"That Jack, he likes you. I could tell."

I frowned. "You could tell, or you were told?"

Nathan shrugged. "Both, I guess. His angel mentioned he only came for a reading so he could get to know you a little better. But that was obvious from his behaviour and all the questions he asked."

"So what? Does it matter?"

"Do you like him?"

I raised an eyebrow. "Are you jealous?" I watched Nathan's expression carefully. He paused for a moment before answering.

"No, it's not that at all." He sighed. "I just–"

The phone rang, making me jump. I looked at my bedside clock. "Who the hell could be ringing at this time?" I grabbed the phone off the bedside table and answered it. "Hello?"

"Marielle?"

The voice was so quiet I barely recognised it. "Sarah? Is that you?" I looked up at Nathan and he was frowning, a concerned look on his face.

"Yes, it's me. I need help."

I had never heard Sarah sounding so scared before, and it was freaking me out. "What is it? What's wrong?"

"I tried one of those exercises from the mediumship book, but something must have gone wrong, and now there's a spirit here, and he's really evil, and I don't know what to do."

I could hear her sobbing down the phone, and I tried to soothe her, but I honestly didn't know what to do. After all, the only spirit I could talk to was Nathan. I wasn't really a medium: I didn't know how to exorcise evil spirits.

"I don't know what to suggest, Sarah. Have you tried protecting yourself, and asking your angels for help?"

"Yes," Sarah whispered. "But he's too strong, and I think he's blocking it. I don't know what he wants but he's got me trapped in my room and I can't get out, and I don't know what to do and–"

"Shhh, it's okay, calm down. He'll be feeding on your fear right now, you need to breathe deeply and stay calm."

There was nothing but the sound of sniffles down the phone, and I looked up at Nathan. Suddenly, I knew what to do. I pressed the mute button on the phone.

"Sarah's in trouble. She tried out a mediumship exercise and she's managed to attract an evil spirit. Can you go to her? Can you help her and protect her?"

Nathan nodded. "I'm sure I can. Will you be okay?"

I waved my hand. "Of course. I'm sure I can sleep alone for a night. Stay with Sarah tonight to make sure it doesn't come back."

Nathan leaned over to kiss me gently. "I love you. I'll be back tomorrow."

"I love you, too."

Nathan disappeared, and I pressed the mute button again.

"Marielle?"

"Yes, I'm here."

"He's gone. The spirit, he's gone." Sarah's voice sounded stronger now, and less fearful. "There's another spirit here now though, a good one. I like this one."

I smiled. "It's Nathan. I sent him to protect you."

"Seriously? Nathan got rid of the spirit for me?"

"Yes, and he will stay with you all night, so try to get some sleep. And for goodness sake, if you're going to call on spirits, could you please put up protection first? And get the angels to make sure only the nice spirits come through?"

Sarah sighed. "Yes, I will, I promise."

"Because you know that doing any of it without protection is like having a sign outside your house saying – 'Party here, free beer' outside, don't you?"

"I know, I know. I'm sorry, it won't happen again, I promise."

"Okay." I softened my tone. "I don't mean to lecture

you, I just don't want you to get hurt, that's all."

"Thank you. I'm sorry I rang so late."

"Don't apologise. You know I am here for you any time of the day."

"Thank you. Night night."

"Night," I echoed. I put the phone down and settled back against my pillow. I reached across to Nathan's side. It was still warm. It had been merely minutes since his departure, but I missed him already.

*   *   *

"So how come you couldn't help her?"

"Her vibration was too low," Sarah's guardian angel answers. Sadness emanates from her as she watches over Sarah's sleeping form.

"I don't understand. Isn't that the point of you guys watching over the humans? So you can clear out the darkness and raise the vibration?"

"That is our intention of course, but it doesn't always work that way. The dark spirits have the ability to lower the vibration and form almost a barrier between us here in the angel dimension, and the humans. It stops us from being able to help. What they call depression is much like this. The negative emotions create a wall that keeps us out. It makes it difficult for us to be effective."

I think about this for a while, but it still doesn't make a lot of sense to me. The angel watches me, she can see my confusion.

"Have you not realised you can connect to source from this dimension?" she asks me.

"Source?"

"As in, the all that is. The universe, God, whatever you wish to name it."

"I'm not sure what you mean."

"You are connected to everything, and everything is connected to you. All the information, emotions, feelings, ideas – anything that exists in the universe – is a part of you, and you are a part of it. If you ever come across something you don't understand, all you need to do is ask the universe, and you will come to know the answer. It will come in the form of a vision, a feeling or simply an understanding."

"Okay, so all I do is ask why angels cannot help humans when their energy is being sucked out and lowered by bad spirits, and I will just know the answer?"

"Yes, that is correct. Try it now," the angel encourages.

Despite all I had experienced and witnessed, this seems a little far out for me, but I decide it wouldn't hurt to try. I ask the question, and become still, allowing my ethereal self to just be. I expand my awareness and allow my soul to connect. I can feel small tendrils of energy all around me, caressing me. I can sense the invisible web that connects every soul together, that connects every soul to the source.

Suddenly, the answer to my question appears before me, as well as the answers to all of my unasked questions. Had I been in human form, it would have been too overwhelming for me to comprehend. But my soul absorbs it all easily, and understands it perfectly. I feel one with everything and everyone, and I can see no reason why anyone, including myself, has ever struggled, or has ever felt alone or isolated.

How do we forget that we are one? That we are all parts of the larger whole? I can also see the lie that is time. I know that time in the angel dimension is very different to the human dimension, but I have not truly understood that time just doesn't exist. It is a way for humans to make sense of their world, but it is just a construct. In truth, everything that has ever happened, ever could happen or that might possibly be happening, all exists in the continuous moment of right now.

I bring my awareness back to the angel dimension, to Sarah's guardian angel. "I think I understand now. But what do I do with all of this knowledge? How do I use it?"

"There's a book called *Infinite You*, which you will give you some practical ideas. You will find it on Marielle's bookshelf."

"You think I should read it?"

"I think you already know what it says, but sometimes it takes the perspective of another to give you a way to use your knowledge."

"Okay. One thing I'm still not sure of is how I was able to get rid of that spirit, and you weren't."

The angel ponders this for a moment. "I think it's because you are able to lower your vibration to match the human dimension quite easily, and therefore you were able to interact with the spirit. They respond to souls who are on a similar vibration to them."

I'm still not sure that makes a whole lot of sense. All I know is that I didn't like the spirit I had evicted. His energy was dark and made me feel queasy, even in my ethereal form. I hope he won't come back to haunt Sarah again.

"What you focus on will surely happen," the angel says, hearing my thoughts. "So focus instead on Sarah being fully protected at all times."

"I think she has learned her lesson on this, don't you?"

The angel chuckles. "I do hope so."

I glance at Sarah's clock on her bedside table, and sigh. I miss being in bed next to Marielle. Despite the fact that I know time does not exist, I know it is going to be a long night.

*   *   *

"What are you reading?"

Nathan looked at me and held the book up. I read the title and shook my head.

"Where did you get it?"

Nathan gestured toward my bookshelf. "From your collection."

I frowned. "Huh, I don't recognise it. Is it any good?"

"It's very interesting," Nathan said. He motioned for me to join him and I went over to the sofa and snuggled up to him. He had lit the fire and it made the cottage cosy in the chilly autumn morning.

"Was Sarah okay this morning?"

Nathan nodded. "Yeah, I waited until she was awake, and made sure there was no sign of the nasty spirit. Her angel said she would let me know if there were any problems again."

"That's good. Thank you for going to look after her. Even though I missed you last night, I appreciate you helping my friend."

Nathan gave me a squeeze. "Any time. At least it's something I can do for you."

I frowned at his tone of voice. "What's that supposed to mean? You do loads for me."

"Only in a spiritual sense."

"Oh, jeez, here we go again. So there are things we will never experience together. So what? There are plenty of couples who never marry or who can't have children. It doesn't matter! Get over it already." Feeling an irrational amount of anger bubble up inside me, I got up from the sofa and went into the kitchen. I didn't want to say something I knew I would regret. I knew Nathan felt bad about not being able to provide those things, but honestly, it just didn't bother me. I wanted him. I wanted us to be together. Nothing else really mattered.

I made a cup of tea and calmed myself down, before going back into the lounge. The book was on the coffee table, but Nathan was gone. I sighed and sat down on the sofa. I picked up the book and started to read where he had left off.

*   *   *

"Is there a parallel universe where I am still alive and Marielle and I get together?"

Marielle's angel looks like he has been expecting me to ask that. His energy is a little sad as he considers how to answer.

"I wondered how long it would take you to figure this out. You connected with source, didn't you?"

"Yes, I did. Now I need to know. Is there a universe where we get together?"

The angel is quiet for a while longer. "You know there is. Anything is possible. There are as many parallel universes as there are past lives and possible futures."

This time it is my turn to be silent. I watch Marielle reading the book. As much as I love being with her, and as much as she says it is enough for her, it isn't enough for me. It just isn't. I want to be human again. I want to have human needs and desires. I want to be able to marry her, to have children with her, to grow old with her. And if there is a possibility of that happening, I have to try.

"What happens in this universe if I enter a different one?"

"It will continue as it is, and the souls within it will continue on the paths they are currently on."

"Can I come back to this universe? If the other universe

doesn't work out?"

"I would assume so. But just as we do not fully understand your ability to switch between the angel dimension and the human dimension, I do not know what the rules are, or whether there are any rules at all. Perhaps you will only be able to switch realities a number of times, or perhaps you could do so endlessly. The only caution I will give you is that you may find you can keep switching, and you might never find a reality that satisfies you, that gives you everything you want, that makes you happy. At some point, you may need to just decide to be happy, no matter what happens."

I'm not really listening by this point. I know the angel is trying to help me, but all I can focus on is how Marielle and I can be together. Properly.

"How do I do it?"

"How do you do anything? You just intend for it to happen. Intend to enter the parallel universe where you are alive and you and Marielle get together, and see what happens."

"Okay. Thank you, I really do appreciate all of your help."

"You're welcome. That's what we are here for."

I allow my awareness to expand again, knowing instinctively I can connect with the reality where Marielle and I are together. I connect with source, and I feel like I have a remote control and am flicking through thousands of channels on a giant TV. When I reach one where I think Marielle and I could be together, I stop and watch for a while. I see myself in my old bedroom at home, I see myself hit a low point, but get through it. One day, instead of going to work, I get in my car and start driving to the university Marielle attends. As I focus on my own self in the car, I feel like I am moving toward the screen, faster and faster until–

*   *   *

"Shit!"

I swerved the car and narrowly missed the rabbit that had hopped into the road. I looked around. I was driving my old car. I waved at the next car that passed by, and they waved back. Other people could see me. I was real.

"Fucking hell!" I yelled. It felt weird to swear, having not done so the entire time I had been dead. Dead. Oh my God, had I really just come back from the dead?

I pulled the car over into the next lay-by, not wanting to cause an accident, and I pinched myself hard. It hurt. I could feel pain. I looked around the car, it felt so strange, like I had never left my body, never left my life. I saw a small black rectangle on the passenger seat and grabbed it. It was my ancient mobile phone. I unlocked it and ignoring the missed call, I found my home number in the contacts list. I pressed the green button and listened to the ringing tone.

"Hello?"

Words stuck in my throat and tears ran down my face. "Mum?" I choked out.

"Nathan? Are you okay? Where are you? The shop rang here asking why you weren't in work this afternoon. They tried your mobile and got no answer. What's going on?"

I smiled at her concern, so glad to hear her voice again. "I'm okay, Mum, everything's okay. There's just someone I need to go visit, and I decided to go and see them instead of going to work. I should have explained before I left, I'm sorry."

"It's okay, as long as you're alright. I'll call the shop and tell them you were feeling unwell so you went to the doctors, okay?"

"Thank you, Mum. I appreciate it. Oh and Mum?" I wiped my tears away with the back of my hand and tried to steady my voice. "I love you."

"Love you too, sweetheart. See you later?"

"Probably. Bye, Mum."

"Bye."

I hung up the phone and shook my head. I still couldn't quite believe I had switched into a parallel universe. Incredible. I looked around and noticed the sun was getting close to setting. At that moment in time, I couldn't remember what day it was, or even what time of year it was. I looked at the time and date on my phone. A memory from the other reality flashed back and I swore again. I needed to get to Marielle, and fast.

Chapter Fifteen

I awoke suddenly, and wondered why it was dark. Had I fallen asleep? Fumbling around for the bedside lamp, I squinted at the clock.

"Oh, crap," I muttered, jumping off the bed. I was still fully clothed, a book fell onto the floor. Ignoring it, I stripped off my clothes and dashed into the bathroom and started trying to freshen myself up.

"Marielle?" There was a knock at the door. "You ready for me to do your makeup?"

I went to the door, and let Sarah in.

"You're still in your underwear?"

I shook my head. "I know, I just lay down for five minutes and fell asleep for three hours. It won't take me long to get ready though."

Sarah walked past me into my room and I took in her outfit. She was wearing a skin-tight black PVC catsuit that showed every curve. The outfit was completed by black stilettos, sultry makeup and bright red fingernails. I whistled. "Wow. That really does not leave much to the imagination."

She did a little twirl. "I know. Do you think I'll get any action tonight?"

"If you don't, every man there must be blind." I started pulling on my more humble black ensemble I had found in my wardrobe. "I, on the other hand, will be happily propping up the bar and people watching."

Sarah frowned. "I think I have some fishnet stockings if you want to borrow them. They'd liven up the outfit a bit. And I have a necklace that would look good on you."

I nodded. "Sure, why not?"

While Sarah went to her room to retrieve the tights and jewellery, I quickly finished dressing and straightened my hair.

"Here you go." Sarah handed me the stockings, and I slipped them on. I didn't own any high heels, so my black boots would have to do. I put the necklace on and looked at myself in the mirror. I looked like I was playing dressing up. I had no idea how women pulled off outfits like this seriously.

"Right. Now sit down while I put some makeup on you. You're as pale as a ghost anyway, so it shouldn't take me long."

With those words, there was a knock at the door.

"Expecting someone?" Sarah asked. I shook my head. She went to answer the door, and I started to apply some bright red lipstick.

"Can I help you?" I heard Sarah ask.

"Sarah, is Marielle there?"

"Uh, yes, do I know you?"

Intrigued by the conversation, I put the lipstick down and went over to the door.

"Nathan," I said in shock. "What brings you here?" I looked up at Nathan's face, pleased to see him, but confused at the same time. We hadn't spoken for a long while. The last time I'd seen him was when he was working in a corner shop, in my hometown. But I had dreamed about him recently.

I noticed him watching me closely and I realised suddenly that I was wearing a revealing outfit, which was very unlike me. I waved at my clothes. "Sarah and I were getting ready for the fetish night at the Union." A thought occurred to me and I looked at Sarah. "How do you know Sarah?"

Nathan frowned. "It's a long story. Look, don't go tonight. Come out for a drink with me instead."

It was my turn to frown. Though we hadn't ever really been close in school, I could tell Nathan wasn't his usual self. "I don't know, I don't want to let Sarah down," I said, looking at my friend.

She shrugged. "It's cool, I know you weren't too excited about going anyway."

I looked back at Nathan. "Okay, could you go and wait in the kitchen while I change into something more appropriate?"

Nathan nodded and headed down the hall, finding the kitchen immediately without needing any directions. Odd. I closed my door and turned to Sarah.

"Are you sure you're okay to go without me?"

"Sure, besides, he's cute! Even if he is a little odd. Is he the one you've been dreaming about recently?"

I nodded. I headed to my wardrobe to find a more suitable outfit. Sarah came to help me, vetoing most of my clothing before allowing me to put on a pair of skinny jeans and a faded blue knit jumper. I went into the bathroom and wiped off the red lipstick, putting on some lip gloss instead. As I got ready, I couldn't stop wondering why he was here.

"Have fun tonight," I said, giving Sarah a hug. "And stay safe."

Sarah chuckled. "I will. See you later."

We left my room together, and she headed out the door, without any kind of coat, crazy woman. After locking my door, I headed for the kitchen. When I saw Nathan sat at the kitchen table, my heart skipped a beat, and I had a strong feeling of déjà vu. I could see a tiny country kitchen, with a tiny table and two chairs, and Nathan sat in one of them. I blinked and the image disappeared.

"You look beautiful," Nathan said.

I laughed. "Bet you preferred the black outfit with fishnets though, huh?"

Nathan shook his head. He stood up and came over to me, then as if it were the most natural thing in the world, he stroked my cheek, then lifted my chin and lowered his lips to mine. My heart stopped for a few seconds when our lips met, and a strong feeling of longing washed over me. I knew I belonged here, in his arms. Our kiss deepened and he pulled me into his embrace. He lifted me up and I wrapped my legs around his waist, not even caring that we were in the dorm kitchen, and that anyone could walk in at any moment.

When we paused to catch our breath, I pulled back a little to look into his dark brown eyes. Again, the feeling of déjà vu washed over me, and I knew I had done this before, that we had been together before. In a past life maybe?

Before I could begin to make sense of it, or even to figure out why he had just turned up at my door out of the blue, we were kissing passionately again.

Without a word, Nathan carried me back to my dorm room, and taking the key from its hiding place (how did he know it was there?) he unlocked the door and carried me inside, our lips barely leaving each other.

He lay me down on my bed, then he lay down beside me. Still without speaking, he wrapped his arms around me and held me close.

My rational mind was screaming at me. This was not normal behaviour. This was a guy I had known years ago, yes, had a bit of a crush on, but had not seen for ages, and who had just turned up out of the blue and started kissing me. And now we were in bed together?

But I ignored all rationality. Being enveloped in Nathan's arms, I felt more at home than I had ever felt anywhere else. I closed my eyes and reached up to kiss him again, wanting the feeling to last forever.

*   *   *

Even though she didn't consciously seem to know why I was there, and believed she hadn't seen me for years, I knew that unconsciously, somewhere within, she knew everything. When we awoke in each other's arms the next day, I wanted to tell her everything, but I was afraid to. What if she thought I was crazy?

She was a little bit shy in the morning. I know that sleeping with someone who was practically a stranger, (though we hadn't done anything but sleep, and kiss, of course) was not what she usually did.

We ate some breakfast, and chatted a little. "Have you spoken to your dad recently?" I asked, before thinking through what I had just said.

Marielle frowned and set her mug down. "No, we haven't spoken in years. Since just after my mum died. Why do you ask?"

My mind was racing. Why had I said that? I shrugged, stalling for time. "I don't know, I just wondered. He must be proud you're in uni now?" I winced internally. I really wasn't good at making stuff up on the spot. I had always been too much of an upfront person.

Marielle shook her head. "No, he couldn't care less."

I knew I should have left the conversation there, but the memory of Marielle being heartbroken that she hadn't contacted her dad before he died was haunting me. I covered her small hand with mine. "Marielle, you know how it was weird, me just turning up yesterday and staying the night, but somehow, it felt right?"

Marielle nodded and blushed a little. "Yes?"

"Please trust me on this. You need to get in touch with your dad." I took my mobile out of my pocket. Ignoring the five missed calls, I dialled in her dad's house number and handed it to her. "Call him."

"How did you even know the number?" She shook her head. "Never mind." She accepted the phone and took a deep breath before pressing the green button.

After a few moments, her eyes locked with mine. "Hey, Dad." She listened for a moment, then tears started to fall. "Oh, Dad. Why didn't you call me earlier?" I took her free hand and squeezed it.

"I can be there in a few hours, Dad. No, it's fine. I need to be there. I'll leave straightaway. Bye."

Marielle hung up the phone and handed it back to me. Without needing any explanation, I stood up and held my hand out to her. "I'll drive you there," I said.

She looked up at me, and nodded before taking my hand.

*   *   *

It seemed as though in a blink of an eye, my whole world had changed. We had arrived at my dad's house to find that he was slipping in and out of consciousness. Nathan got him into the car, and drove us to the nearest hospital. I didn't even question how Nathan knew where my dad lived, or where everything was, I was focused entirely on my father.

I knew we had never seen eye-to-eye, but he was my dad. And I loved him. I rode in the back with him, holding him tightly while Nathan drove. We arrived at A&E and Nathan ran in to get someone. Everything moved in slow motion as they came out to the car and wheeled my father into A&E. They took him directly to a bed and started checking him over. He wasn't very responsive at this point, and my heart was hammering.

Once they had done what they needed to do to stabilise him, I found myself alone with him for a few moments. Nathan had gone to park the car.

"Dad?" I whispered. I held his hand gently, and smoothed his straggly fringe away from his forehead. When had he got so old? It had only been a few years since I'd seen him last, but he looked decades older.

"Marielle?" His eyes opened and he looked straight at me.

"I'm here, Dad. I'm here." I squeezed his hand, and he squeezed mine in return.

He smiled, making him instantly look younger, more like the man I remembered.

"I was so worried you wouldn't come." A tear glistened in the corner of his eye. I had never, in my whole life, seen him cry. "I dreamed you didn't call me, you didn't come. And I died without being able to say goodbye."

My own eyes filled up. "Shh, it was just a dream. I'm here. I love you."

My father smiled again, his eyes closed and his body relaxed. I watched him closely, afraid he was just going to slip away.

"Ms Gibson?"

I looked up to see the doctor standing there, a clipboard in his hands. Nathan was just behind him. "May I have a word?"

I kissed my father on the forehead, then pulled my hand away from his. "I'll be right back," I whispered. I followed the doctor out into the hallway, and he led me to his office. Nathan came with me.

"Are you family?" the doctor asked Nathan as we sat down.

"He's my boyfriend," I said, without thinking about it. I looked over at Nathan, who was holding my hand. He smiled and gave me a tiny nod.

"I'm afraid your father's cancer has metastasized. He has maybe a few days, a week at most, I would say."

I felt Nathan's grip tighten on my hand but nothing else felt real. "A week?" I whispered.

"Yes. We will make him as comfortable as possible, but really, there is nothing else we can do for him."

I nodded. Asking further questions seemed pointless. "Thank you. Can I go back to him now?"

The doctor nodded. The walk back to my dad's cubicle seemed to stretch on forever. Before we reached it, I stopped and turned to Nathan. "You knew, didn't you?"

Nathan sighed. "Yes. I did."

"But how? How did you know he was ill, and where he lived? I don't understand."

"It's a long story, and quite frankly, I don't think you would believe me. The main thing is now you have a chance to say goodbye."

Without warning, the floodgates opened and I was unable to stop it. I sobbed, and Nathan pulled me into his arms, not saying a word, but holding me tightly, making me feel like he would never let go.

*   *   *

Just as before, there were just the two of us at the funeral. Only this time, the vicar could see us both.

The weeks passed by much as they had in the other

reality, we cleaned out her father's cottage, and moved in there. Only this time, I found a job so I could support us. Marielle got part-time work in the café. Interestingly, in this reality, Charlotte did not work there. And no one in the village had heard of her. I wondered where she was and whether she had become an actress.

Life ticked by comfortably, we mainly kept to ourselves in the tiny cottage, and after Marielle's grief had subsided, we were happy. We went out for long walks, went out for the occasional meal or to the cinema in the next town. Sarah came to visit a couple of times, and she commented that despite the bizarre beginning to our relationship, she couldn't imagine two people better suited to one another. I kept in touch with my family, though it had taken them a little while to come to terms with the fact that I suddenly had a serious relationship and was moving away. They had met Marielle though, and I knew they approved and were happy for me.

Six months later, I was lying in bed, reading *Infinite You*, when Marielle came in from the bathroom, looking a little pale.

"What's wrong?" I asked her, putting the book down. "Are you okay?"

"Yeah, I must have eaten something off at the café today. I just threw up."

"Come here," I pulled the covers aside and Marielle climbed in next to me. I pulled her close. "Do you want me to get you some water?"

Marielle shook her head and nestled into my arms. "I just need sleep."

"Okay." I reached over her to switch the light off, and I watched her fall asleep in the moonlight. For some reason, fear was gripping me. In the other reality, she had never been ill, not once. I prayed to her angels to make her well again, then I fell asleep too.

*   *   *

I leaned against the thin wall of the café toilet cubicle and stared at the small white stick in shock.

I was pregnant.

I must have stared at it for a good fifteen minutes before a hammering on the door brought me back to reality.

"Marielle! Are you in there?"

Shaking myself out of my stupor, I wrapped the test up in toilet paper and put it in the bin before washing my hands. I went back out to the café, and apologised to the manager. I grabbed my pen and paper, and started taking people's orders. I worked on auto-pilot for the rest of the day, and just about managed to get away with not being told off again. After work, I sat in my car and stared out of the window.

Pregnant. I'd never really wanted children. It wasn't something I was desperate to do. And Nathan and I had only been together for a few months. It was hardly a stable relationship. We earned enough to cover the bills and luckily there was no mortgage on the house, but still. Having kids was an expensive thing to do.

And did Nathan even want children? We had never discussed it. Goodness, we hadn't even discussed the nature of our relationship or even marriage, let alone having children.

Beginning to feel queasy again, and a little panicked, I forced myself to breathe deeply. After a few minutes, I felt calm enough to turn on the ignition and drive home.

Nathan was cooking in the kitchen, when I arrived back at the cottage. As I stepped through the door, another strong feeling of déjà vu washed over me, and the feeling of familiarity hit me over the head. Despite my reservations, I knew that our relationship felt right to me. And I knew we could figure things out.

"Hey, you. I got home a little earlier so I thought I'd surprise you."

I stepped into the kitchen and Nathan pulled me into his arms. But the smell of onions and garlic made me feel sick, and retching, I pulled away from him and ran for the bathroom. I only just made it in time to lose my lunch down the toilet. I heard Nathan come into the room.

"You're seriously making me dubious about ever eating in the café again," he joked.

I wiped my mouth on the towel and flushed the toilet. I closed the lid and sat down on it.

"Nathan," I looked up at him, and my serious expression made him lose his grin. He came over and knelt down in front of me, taking my hands in his.

"What is it?"

I sighed. "I'm pregnant."

His eyes widened and his mouth opened and closed several times. Suddenly, he grinned and squeezed my hands. "Are you serious?"

I nodded. "Yes, I am."

He pulled me to my feet and crushed me to his chest. Then he lifted me up and kissed me, ignoring the fact that my breath stank. I pulled back a little. "You're okay with this?" I asked.

"Okay? I'm ecstatic!" He grinned again. "Aren't you excited?"

I shrugged. "I guess. I just haven't processed it properly yet. I mean, well…" I swallowed hard, and felt fear bubbling up to the surface. "I guess I'm just a little scared."

Nathan frowned. "Scared? Why?" He carried me into

the bedroom and sat on the bed, with me on his lap.

I shook my head. "It's nothing rational. I've just always had this weird fear of giving birth, that's all."

Nathan smiled. "I'm sure a lot of women have the same fear. It'll all be fine, you'll see."

"I'm sure it will be." I smiled back, and began to feel a glimmer of excitement. "So are we really going to do this? Are we really going to have a child?"

"Yes, we are. But there is something I need to do first, something I have wanted to do since the moment we got together, but didn't want to scare you away."

"Which is?"

Nathan stood up and turned around to place me on the bed, then he went over to his chest of drawers. After a few moments of rummaging, he pulled something out and came back to me. The second before he knelt down on one knee, I realised what he was about to do. I bit my lip.

"Marielle, I know we are fated to be together. Will you marry me?"

The fact that he already had a ring reassured me that he wasn't just proposing because I was pregnant and felt he had a duty to so. I still couldn't explain our connection, but I did know I didn't want to be with anyone else.

"Yes, I will."

Chapter Sixteen

As we planned the wedding and decorated the tiny second bedroom in bright colours, thoughts and memories of the other realities faded away. Occasionally I found myself waking up in the morning feeling as though I had been talking to beings on the other side, and I'd have a feeling that things weren't quite right. But then I would open my eyes and see Marielle's face, and reach out to feel her growing belly, and all of those thoughts would be driven away, to be forgotten until I slept and dreamed again.

We wanted to get married before she was showing too much, and we both agreed on something simple. So we booked a registry office service, back in the seaside town where we grew up together, for just four weeks later. My family were over the moon, and didn't seem to mind at all that Marielle was pregnant. Marielle had invited Sarah, and a couple of old school friends including Jane, but it was a very small affair. Afterwards, we all had afternoon tea in a local café and chatted to our guests.

In the early evening, I suggested we go for a stroll on the beach.

"I haven't been back here in years," Marielle said, staying close to my side as the cool sea breeze rippled past us.

"Up until I came to find you, I would spend every spare moment I had here," I said, watching the waves as we walked across the sand.

"You know, you've never explained it to me. Why you suddenly came to find me. Even your mum told me she was shocked. She said you just took off one day, with no word to anyone. You blew off work and came to find me." She stopped walking and turned to face me. "What made you do that?"

For a moment, I couldn't even remember. Memories of my life before Marielle were hazy and vague. A vision flashed in my mind of being in the angel dimension, of looking for the parallel universe where we got to be together. I blinked and focused on her face. I knew she was waiting for an answer, but I couldn't possibly tell her the truth. She would think I was completely insane.

"I guess I realised how I felt about you, and I took a risk that you might feel the same way." I shouldn't have worried. My pathetic, made up reason was just as ridiculous as the real one.

"I didn't think you ever looked at me that way, in school, I mean. And I certainly didn't think you knew I had a crush on you, but I guess you must have, on some level."

Marielle didn't seem to be suspicious, and I relaxed a little.

"I guess I must have picked up on it. I know it was an impulsive and mad thing to do, just getting in my car and driving to come and see you, but there was something in my gut telling me I had to."

She smiled at me, and I knew I was off the hook for now. We continued our walk down the beach, and I inhaled the salty air, enjoying the feel and smell of the sea. I missed being near the water. Though our cottage was quite far inland, I decided we should make time to take day trips to the sea, because I knew I would want our child to spend plenty of time on the coast.

When we reached the water's edge, we stopped again, and I wrapped my arms around her. She looked up at me, staring into my eyes. The world could have ended right then and there, and I wouldn't have noticed.

"I can't believe we just got married," I whispered.

Her smile grew wider. "I can. Though I'm amazed we managed to organise it in such a short space of time."

I nodded. "Perhaps you should go into business organising last-minute weddings," I joked.

She raised an eyebrow. "Do you know what? That's not a bad idea." She looked at my expression of horror and laughed. "I'm joking. Don't worry, I have no intention of organising another wedding for a long time." She rested her hand on her stomach. "Besides, I'll have plenty to keep me busy in just a few months."

I smiled and placed my hand over hers. "We both will."

*   *   *

Time seemed to fly by after we got married. It was like life was on fast-forward. Christmas came and went, the new year arrived in a quiet fashion, and suddenly I couldn't even fit into the maternity clothes I had reluctantly bought. Standing in the bathroom one morning, I looked into the mirror and didn't even recognise my own face. My cheeks were fuller, I had bags under my eyes from lack of sleep (and I couldn't even begin to imagine how little sleep I would get once the baby was born) and my skin seemed ridiculously pale. Why did we live in England? Why couldn't we live somewhere hotter and sunnier?

Making my way down the stairs at a snail's pace, holding my huge bump steady, I reminded myself that I really was a very lucky woman. I felt even luckier when I reached the kitchen and found Nathan there, making me breakfast. He was the sweetest and most attentive and loving man I had ever known, and though I still didn't fully understand why he had decided to come and find me all those months ago, I was very glad he had.

Feeling quite emotional now, tears began streaming down my cheeks without me really noticing it. Nathan heard me and turned, a smile on his face and a plate of pancakes in his hand. When he saw my tears he put the plate down quickly and moved toward me.

"What is it? Are you okay? Has it started?"

The baby was due at any moment, and I knew that as excited as he was, Nathan was also concerned for me. Though I had kept most of my fears to myself, they would occasionally rise to the surface and I would have a day of crying uncontrollably.

"I'm okay," I said, breathing deeply and trying to smile. "Just feeling a bit emotional. And tired."

Nathan led me over to the table and helped me into the chair. "Didn't you sleep very well again last night?"

I shook my head. "I just couldn't get comfortable. And when I did finally fall asleep, I got too hot and had nightmares."

Nathan frowned. "Oh, sweetie, I'm sorry. Maybe you should have a nap later."

"I probably will. It's not like I can do much else at this point."

Nathan served my breakfast with a flourish, and though I didn't really feel like eating, I made an attempt to because he had gone to so much trouble. He sat opposite me and tucked into his own pancakes.

"What time are you working today?" I never seemed to remember when his shifts were, especially at the moment, my memory was just terrible.

"I need to be there by nine. But only if you're feeling

okay. If you're not feeling good I can call in and say I need the day off."

"No, no, I'll be fine, I'm just going to take it easy, maybe read a book or watch a movie. You don't need to stay and babysit me."

"Call me if there is anything you need or if it starts, okay?"

"Of course." I picked at my pancakes, taking tiny bites. Nathan finished his and gulped down his juice.

"Do you need anything before I leave?"

I shook my head and he stood up from the table, came over to kiss me on the forehead then he put his dishes in the sink. "Leave the dishes, I'll do them later, okay?"

I nodded again and he left the kitchen. I stared at my empty mug, wondering what I could do with myself. As much as I feared giving birth, I had to admit, I was getting bored of being pregnant. It felt like my life had been paused, and I couldn't press play again until the baby was born.

Nathan came back into the kitchen to say goodbye, then he left for work, leaving me alone in the kitchen. I stopped trying to eat the pancakes, and poured myself a second cup of tea instead. I took my mug into the lounge, set it on the coffee table, and after putting some music on, I sat on the sofa, and leaned back into the cushions.

Without even meaning to, I closed my eyes and fell asleep.

*   *   *

Even before I felt my mobile phone vibrating in my pocket, I knew something was wrong. I could feel it through the strong bond Marielle and I shared. I felt a pain rip through my stomach that made me gasp, and a second later my phone went. I fumbled with it, trying to get it out of my pocket and press the green button. I didn't even bother to check the screen, I knew it was Marielle. Before she had even started speaking I had dropped everything and was walking toward the exit.

"Nathan," she gasped. My heart clenched at the sound of the panic in her voice.

"Have you rung an ambulance?" I asked, not even bothering to wait for her to say anything else.

"No," she said.

"I'm going to hang up, call an ambulance, and I will call you back immediately, I'm on my way now, okay?"

"Okay." Her voice was barely a whisper now, and my heart was thudding so hard it hurt. I hung up and called an ambulance as I unlocked my car and got in. I was driving down the motorway when I called her back. She answered, but all I could hear was her shallow breathing.

"The ambulance is on its way, and I'm on my way. Stay with me, okay? Just stay with me. Everything is going to be fine. Please, just stay with me." The pain ripped through my stomach again, making me gasp, and Marielle gasped simultaneously. I struggled to keep the car on the road, and knew that if I were to be stopped by the police, I would probably lose my licence. Doing ninety while talking on a mobile phone and not wearing a seatbelt? Definitely a driving ban waiting to happen.

I kept talking, about stupid things, pointless things, trying to keep her alert, and trying to keep myself from panicking further. But she was barely responding to anything I said, and when I finally pulled my car up behind the ambulance outside the cottage, I was fearing the worst.

I jumped out of the car, and ran up the path, nearly ripping the front door of its hinges. I could see the paramedics in the lounge, and I stopped suddenly in the doorway. There was a pool of blood on the floor. Suddenly I wanted to gag. I felt bile rise up to my throat and I fought to stay calm. I went around the paramedics to Marielle's side and saw that she was already unconscious. The male paramedic noticed my presence and started peppering me with questions, but I didn't know how to answer most of them.

"Has she got any medical conditions? Is she on any medication? How far gone is she?"

"The baby, the baby is due now," I said. "Why is she bleeding? What's going on?"

The paramedic muttered something to the female and she went out to the ambulance to get the stretcher. Everything became a blur as they lifted her onto the stretcher – which only just fit through the tiny cottage door – and took her out to the ambulance. By the time I had gathered myself and grabbed the ready-packed bag and locked the cottage and followed them, they had already hooked her up to all sorts of machines. I got into the back of the ambulance and we sped away, sirens blaring and lights flashing. I felt numb.

I stared at Marielle's pale face, covered with an oxygen mask, and I didn't know what to do. The paramedic worked around me, mostly ignoring me, only asking me brief questions that yet again, I had no answer to. "We've only been together for a year," I whispered. Finally I moved forward and touched her hand, which was as cold as it was pale. I took it in mine and squeezed it gently, looking for a response, any response, but there was none.

"Is the baby going to be okay?" I asked, staring at the bump that seemed so much bigger than it was this morning.

"We need to get her to hospital as soon as possible. The fact that she has lost a lot of blood and is unconscious is very worrying, we need to get her there and have the baby delivered immediately by Caesarean section."

His words did not reassure me. I gripped her hand tighter, and started to pray. My vague memories of being in between worlds came back to me, and I began to whisper to Marielle's guardian angel, to mine, to God, to anyone who was listening to my thoughts, to make sure she would be okay, and to make sure that the baby would be okay, too.

The journey to the hospital seemed to stretch out for eternity and yet last only a few moments. We came to a stop and there was another blur of motion as they took Marielle straight into theatre. I just about got the chance to kiss her on the forehead before she was wheeled away, and I was left to sit in the noisy waiting room.

I continued to pray, not caring that others around me thought I was an insane man, muttering to himself. I didn't move from my seat until I heard my name being called.

When I looked up to meet the eyes of the doctor in front of me, I knew she was gone. I dropped my head back into my hands and sobbed.

*　　　*　　　*

It's a weird feeling, floating above my body, pale and lifeless below me. I hear the cries of my newborn child and the joy I feel at the sight of her beautiful face is marred only by the fact that I will never hold her. Even as they fight to save me, and try to get my heart to re-start, I know it is too late. I won't be going back. I move over to my daughter, and I marvel at her perfect beauty. I can see Nathan in her nose, in her expression, and I can see myself in the shape of her face and her lips. I know it will break Nathan's heart to lose me, but at least he has this perfect blend of us both to keep him going.

When the medical team finally all agree upon what I have known for several minutes, they set about cleaning up my body, so Nathan can say goodbye to me, I assume. They take my baby away, and I try to follow, but find I can't. I don't have to wait too long before the door opens again, and my beautiful husband enters. His face is red and his eyes look sore. Tears stream openly down his cheeks as he approaches my bedside.

For a long time, he stands by the side of the bed and finally, he reaches out to touch my face. I move to his side and try to take his hand. To my surprise, he looks down at his hand, as though he can feel my touch.

"Nathan," I say. "Nathan, I'm here."

"He cannot hear you."

I look up to see a beautiful being watching me. "Who are you?"

"I am your guardian angel. I have come to take you home."

I look at Nathan, who is sobbing. "I can't leave him yet, he needs me."

The angel shakes his head. "I'm afraid it's time for you to go home. He will understand, you'll see."

I nod and reach up to kiss Nathan on the cheek. He closes his eyes and his sobs subside a little. Then he leans forward to kiss my cold, lifeless lips.

"I love you so much," he whispers to my still body.

"I love you too," I reply.

After a few moments, he straightens up and leaves the room without looking back.

"Will he take care of my child?" I ask the angel.

"Yes, I will make sure of it."

"Okay, I guess I'm ready to go."

The angel moves toward me, and opens his arms. I step

into his embrace, and am surrounded by a pure white light, and absolute, unconditional love.

*   *   *

Was it my fault?

Had I caused Marielle's death by switching to another parallel universe? Would she still be living if I hadn't suddenly entered her life, married her and got her pregnant?

I looked down at the perfectly formed child sleeping in my arms, and a sigh shuddered through me. But if I had not done any of those things, this beautiful being would not exist. I rocked her gently, and walked over to the window where the sun was rising, filling the room with an orange glow. The sun's rays shone upon her tiny face, illuminating her beautiful lips that were the same shape as Marielle's.

The image of Marielle's cold, still body flashed through my mind and I struggled to breathe. Why did she have to leave me? How could I possibly look after a tiny baby by myself? How could I live alone in the cottage?

I pondered these things while I watched the sun rise, glancing down every few seconds at my sleeping child, and a long-forgotten conversation resurfaced in my mind.

"Can I come back to this universe? If the other universe doesn't work out?"

"I would assume so. The only caution I will give you is that you may find you can keep switching, and you might never find a reality that satisfies you, that gives you everything you want, that makes you happy. At some point, you may need to just decide to be happy, no matter what happens."

"How do I do it?"

"How do you do anything? You just intend for it to happen.

Intend to enter the parallel universe where you are alive and you and Marielle are together, and see what happens."

I turned away from the window, went back to the cot, and lay my baby girl down in it, making sure she was snug inside her pink blanket.

"I know you'll be okay," I whispered. "Goodbye, my darling." I leaned down to kiss her tiny forehead, then crossed the room to the window. I stared at the light of the sun for a few moments before closing my eyes and willing my soul to return to the universe where Marielle was alive and well, and I was a spirit again.

$$* \qquad * \qquad *$$

"Hello, Nathan."

I open my eyes and look up at the guardian angel standing over my child. I look back at the window, and see myself. I turn back to the angel.

"What will happen to this version of myself? To my child?"

"They will continue their lives. I will continue to watch over your child. Who you will name Snowdrop, in memory of Marielle's mother."

I feel the lingering grief in my soul. "What about the other universe? The one where Marielle is alive, and I am a spirit? Does it still exist?"

"Of course. But if you were to re-enter it now, I do not think you would do so at the point in time in which you left."

I feel confused. "What do you mean?"

"Things in that universe have moved along. You went back in time when you entered this universe, but I do not know if you will be able to go back in time when you go back to the other universe."

His explanation confuses me further, and I can feel the human emotion of impatience sweeping over me.

"It doesn't really matter. Can I go back?"

"Seeing as we are having this conversation, and you are in the angel dimension, I would say you already were back. You just need to return to Marielle."

"Yes, right, of course." I look at my baby one more time, then I close my eyes, and think of my beautiful soul mate.

Chapter Seventeen

For a few moments after opening my eyes, I felt disorientated. My dreams had been vivid and realistic, and for a moment I expected to be somewhere other than my own bed in the cottage. I felt strong arms encircle me from behind and I smiled, my reality rushing back to me.

"Good morning."

I turned to face Jack. "Good morning yourself."

"Did you sleep okay? You seemed to be tossing and turning a lot."

I frowned. "I'm sorry, I hope I didn't disturb you too much. I was having some really odd dreams."

Jack propped himself up on his elbow. "About what?"

I thought for a moment, and flashes of myself and Nathan together, of us getting married and having a child went through my mind. I looked into Jack's eyes. "I can't remember now, I just remember they were vivid."

"I hate it when that happens. When you know you've had some crazy dreams but you can't remember them."

I nodded in agreement. I didn't like lying to Jack, but I didn't see the point in bringing up Nathan now. I lay back in Jack's arms, and before I could stop myself, I wondered for the millionth time where Nathan was.

I remembered the day he left, and the days that followed, waiting for him to come back. I talked out loud to him every day, telling him that I hadn't meant to get mad at him, I hadn't wanted him to leave. But there had been no response. Time went on, and I found myself in front of a roomful of people at the next event Donna had organised. My cheeks reddened at the awful memory.

"I'm sorry," I had told the audience after sitting in front of them for ten cringing minutes. "I'm just not getting any messages through tonight." I was in shock that Nathan hadn't turned up. Even if he was mad at me, how could he hurt and embarrass me in this way? I had felt sure he would swoop in and save the day, but he didn't.

"Don't worry, I will make sure you are all reimbursed for your ticket costs," I had mumbled over the irritated chatter. I stood up and as I tried to leave, the crowd turned ugly.

"We drove for two hours to get here tonight," someone had called out. "Are you going to give us back our fuel expenses too?"

"I need to hear from my dad, is my dad okay?" another voice had screamed.

Suddenly a pair of arms wrapped round me and guided me out of the room, to the safety of my car. I had looked up to see Jack, though I had irrationally hoped it would be Nathan.

He got my keys out of my bag, as I stood there shaking, and he opened the car. He gently pushed me into the passenger seat and got into the driver's side, before pulling out of the car park. I looked up to see the angry mob spilling out of the village hall and I started to cry.

"Don't worry, they'll get over it," he had said.

"He's gone," I had whispered. "He's really gone."

"Earth to Marielle, come in, Marielle."

I pulled myself out of my memory and looked up at Jack. "Sorry, I was lost in thought. What did you say?"

"I asked if you were working today?"

I scanned my memory for my schedule, and shook my head. "No, I've got an afternoon shift tomorrow and a full day on Friday. Why?"

"Because I happen to have the day off, and I was hoping I could take you out for the day."

I smiled. "That sounds lovely. Where are we going?"

"Ah, I'm afraid that's a secret. Just get yourself ready, we should leave in an hour."

"Okay." I reached up to give him a kiss and hopped out of bed and made my way to the shower. While the hot water streamed down on me, I thought about what a godsend Jack had been in the last few months. The fact that Nathan was really gone had hit me hard.

If it hadn't been for Jack, I knew I would have slipped into a depression. It wasn't like a normal break up. I couldn't write to him, call or text him, or even go and find him. For all I knew, Nathan had moved onto the other side, to another dimension, and I might never see him again.

I shook off the dark thoughts and concentrated on getting myself ready. I had been working a lot lately, after getting a job in the café where Charlotte had worked. She had finally listened to her grandmother's advice, and two months ago, she had broken up with her husband, quit her job and moved back to London. We chatted on the phone regularly, she had already got a couple of small parts in soap operas, and was currently auditioning for theatre roles. I was pleased for her, and I knew her grandmother would be too.

She knew I was looking for work after the mediumship gig had come to a sudden halt, so she had recommended me to the owner of the café. It was easy work, and I enjoyed the interaction with the customers, but I knew it wasn't my life's purpose to serve tea and cake.

The problem was, I had no idea what my life's purpose was.

I came out of the bathroom to find a tray on the bed. I smiled when I saw the single red rose next to the tea and pancakes. Jack always went out of his way to do sweet things for me. I racked my brain, and tried to think if today was some kind of anniversary I had forgotten about, but I didn't think so.

Less than an hour later, we were in Jack's car, heading west. He still wouldn't tell me where we were going.

"Just a hint, please?" I asked.

He shook his head, not taking his eyes off the road ahead. "Nope. You'll just have to wait and see."

I smiled and gave up. I leaned back in my seat and watched the scenery whizzing past. A couple of hours later, we reached the coastline, and Jack pulled up in a small car park by the beach.

"We're here," he announced.

"We are?" I asked. I looked around, not recognising the beach.

"You're always saying how you miss the sea, having grown up near it, so I thought you would enjoy a trip to the seaside."

"It's true. I do miss it." I took my seatbelt off and leaned over to kiss him. "Thank you."

"You're welcome. Now let's go for a walk on the beach and then have a wander through the town."

I got out of the car, and despite it being a sunny, spring day, the cool sea breeze made me glad I had put on a jumper. I pulled the sleeves down over my hands, and went to join Jack.

We made our way down to the sand, where I took my shoes and socks off so I could feel the sand between my toes.

A sudden feeling of déjà vu slammed through me, and I looked down at my stomach and saw a small bump under a cream dress. I looked up at Jack, and instead saw Nathan's dark hair and eyes. Blinking rapidly, I turned to look at the sea. When I looked back, everything was back to normal again.

"Are you okay?" Jack asked, noticing my small episode.

I nodded slowly. "I think so. Just a really strong déjà vu."

"Another one?"

I frowned. I guess I'd had perhaps more feelings of déjà vu than normal in the last few months. "It's passed now, I'm sure it was nothing."

"Has Nathan ever come back?" he asked. I could tell from the tone of his voice that he had been wanting to ask the question for a while. Hearing him mention Nathan out loud, just seconds after seeing Nathan's face instead of his, made me feel a little unsteady on my feet and I abruptly sat down on the damp sand.

Jack sat down next to me, and was silent for a while. Though I had never explained the full extent of my relationship with Nathan, he knew we had shared a strong bond, and that I still missed him. I knew it couldn't be easy for him to feel like he was continually competing with a ghost.

"No," I said finally. "He has never come back."

"Do you want him to?"

I sighed. "No. I think he has moved on. Gone into the light, or onto the next level, or whatever it is spirits are meant to do. And I wouldn't want him to come back now."

"Not even to help you do the mediumship again?"

I shook my head. "No, I never really felt comfortable doing that. I felt like one day someone would find out the truth and I would be seen as a fraud." I laughed. "And I guess that's exactly what ended up happening."

Jack was silent for a few moments, then he clapped his hands, making me jump. "Okay, this conversation is getting way too serious, let's go get some ice cream! I might even treat you to a flake if you're good."

I laughed. "Sounds good to me."

Jack got to his feet then reached down to grab my hand and pull me up. We walked back toward the town. He held my hand tightly as we walked, and I felt safe by his side. I glanced back at the waves crashing onto the sand, and smiled.

Goodbye, Nathan, I thought, sending my words out into the universe in the hope that he would hear me. *Maybe I'll see you again one day.*

*   *   *

I watch Marielle turn away from me, and walk away with her new lover. "Goodbye," I echo, knowing she isn't listening.

"He's going to propose to her," Marielle's guardian angel tells me.

I nod. "I know. I can see it in his eyes." I turn to the angel. "What I don't understand is why I disappeared from this life. I thought you said this universe would continue as before. What happened?"

The angel is thoughtful for a moment. "It would seem that by drawing your consciousness into another parallel universe, you actually withdrew your consciousness entirely from this universe." The angel sighs. "As I said before, there are no rules, no guidelines. I warned you I did not know how it would turn out. And that ultimately, you could keep searching forever, keep switching and living different realities, but never really find one that makes you happy, or turns out the way you want it to. Really, the only solution is to be happy with what you have, in the moment you are in."

"So you think I should be happy, and accept that we won't be together?"

"I cannot tell you what you should accept or be happy with. I can only make suggestions. You have free will to do as you choose."

I'm quiet for a while. Marielle and Jack have long since disappeared, and I feel an emptiness in my ethereal heart. I know the angel is right. I can keep searching for the perfect universe for the rest of eternity, but ultimately, in my desperate search, I'm likely to miss out on the only thing that matters, which is the present.

"Perhaps you could make some suggestions about what I should do now," I say.

"Actually, there was something I had in mind, which you might be interested in."

"I'm listening."

Epilogue

My hands were shaking as I tried to put my earrings in, and I felt a warm hand patiently take the small stud out of my hand and put it in for me. I smiled up in thanks at Sarah.

"Why are you so nervous? That man is hot," Charlotte said, from her place behind me, doing my hair.

I smiled. "I don't know, it just feels weird, I suppose. I'm not used to having this much fuss made over me. It's just making me nervous."

"How about we finish your transformation and then we leave you alone to have a bit of chill out time?" Sarah said.

I nodded, much to Charlotte's annoyance as she tried to pin my hair in place. "Yes, that would be good. Thank you." I smiled in the mirror at them both. "You guys look gorgeous, by the way."

Charlotte grinned back. "I know."

I laughed, and felt some of the tension and nervousness slip away. By the time they had finished, I was feeling calmer. They helped me step into my dress, and buttoned me up. A few minutes later, I was alone in the hotel room.

"You look beautiful."

I spun around and nearly fainted in shock. "Nathan," I mouthed, no sound coming out.

He smiled his beautiful smile and my heart thudded. It had been years since the day he left, never to be seen again, yet here he was, on my wedding day, looking like he'd been there the whole time.

"What took you guys so long? He proposed to you years ago."

I ignored his question and the fact that he knew when Jack had proposed. "Where have you been?" I demanded, suddenly finding my voice. All of the grief and hurt and rejection resurfaced from the dark hole I had buried it in and I moved toward him, wishing I could make him understand how awful I had felt when he had never returned.

His smile disappeared. "Oh, you know," he said. "Just off saving the world."

I frowned. "What do you mean?"

"I've been helping people who are depressed and surrounded by evil spirits. Seems I have a knack for moving the spirits on and freeing people from their grasp."

I raised my eyebrows. "Really? And you couldn't say goodbye first before dashing off to be a superhero spirit? Did I really mean so little to you?"

Nathan looked like I had slapped him across the face. "You mean everything to me," he whispered, all trace of humour gone. "I didn't mean to leave you, I was trying to make things better. But it didn't work. When I came back, you were with Jack, and you said you wouldn't want me to come back, you said goodbye."

My conversation with Jack on the beach came back to me. "You were there. I knew you were there. Why didn't you show yourself? Why didn't you at least say goodbye to me?"

Nathan shook his head. "I don't know. I didn't think it would help. I didn't want to take you away from Jack, you seemed happy."

"I was happy," I muttered. I sat down on the bed, feeling tired all of a sudden. I didn't care about creasing the back of my silk dress. Nathan sat next to me.

"So why has it taken you guys so long to get hitched?"

I shrugged. "We weren't in a hurry, I guess. I realised what I wanted to do with my life, which meant going back to college–"

"To do what?" Nathan interrupted.

"It occurred to me that even though I could no longer connect people to their loved ones, I could actually train to help people who are grieving. So I decided to become a grief counsellor."

Nathan was quiet for a while, then he nodded. "I can see you being good at that."

"I did it for myself as much as anyone else. I needed to learn how to get over losing you," I whispered. I looked at Nathan, and he had closed his eyes, his expression pained.

He opened his eyes and looked at me. "I'm so sorry for leaving you," he whispered.

"So why did you? And why have you come back now?" I asked, my sadness giving way to anger. Nathan moved from the bed next to me to his knees on the carpet in front of me. He reached up to take my hands, and they tingled at his touch.

"I want another chance," he said.

To say I was shocked would have been a massive understatement. "You what?"

"I know it was stupid of me to leave, and I know I don't deserve another chance, but I am here to ask you for one, because I love you. I know I was meant to be with you, and you know you were meant to be with me."

I stood up and shook my hands loose, shaking with rage that had developed from my grief. "You left me five years ago. Five years! After a stupid argument you just disappeared and never came back. And now you just appear again, on my WEDDING DAY, to ask for a

SECOND CHANCE?" I knew I shouldn't shout, that people might be able to hear me in the adjoining rooms, but I didn't care. So what if they thought I was a crazy woman?

Nathan stayed kneeling on the floor and hung his head. Part of me wanted to apologise for my outburst, and throw myself into his arms. Why the hell did I still love him so much? Why did I want him? It just made no sense.

"I can't, Nathan," I said, my voice calmer and quieter. "I just can't. There is a man waiting for me at the end of the aisle who would do anything for me. Anything. There is no way I am going to lose him, and come back to you, only to be abandoned again."

Nathan nodded, still not looking up to meet my eyes. "I understand."

"I think you should go."

After a moment, Nathan stood and finally looked me in the eye. "I never intended to hurt you. But in my selfishness, I did anyway. I will never be able to take that back, and I'm sorry. I really do hope you and Jack are happy together."

I nodded. Tears were welling up in my eyes, but I tried to hold them back. I knew Sarah would never forgive me for ruining the makeup she spent ages applying.

Nathan touched the side of my face, then leaned down to kiss my forehead. "I love you."

I couldn't answer. I stared down at the carpet, which blurred as tears filled my eyes. After a few moments, when I looked up, he was gone. I collapsed back onto the bed and cried.

*   *   *

"Marielle? Jesus, what did she do to her makeup?"

I opened my eyes and blinked at the face staring at me, not recognising it for a moment.

"When we left you to chill out, we didn't mean for you to fall asleep."

I felt a tug and Charlotte's hands were in my hair, teasing it back into place. I felt Sarah's brushes on my face, sorting out my makeup. Somehow, I was sat in the chair at the dressing table. I looked more closely at myself in the mirror. My eyes weren't red or puffy. I didn't look like I'd been crying, yet my last memory was of Nathan leaving and me crying myself to sleep, on the bed... I looked over to the smooth covers of the bed in confusion. Had it not been real? Had I really fallen asleep and dreamed the whole thing?

"What is it? You look like you're trying to work out some incredibly complicated problem," Sarah said.

I frowned and shook my head. "It's nothing, I just had a really vivid dream, I guess."

"It's time to go, beautiful. We don't want to keep that man of yours waiting."

I smiled at Charlotte, and shook off the lingering memory of Nathan's lips touching my forehead. "You're right. Let's do this."

I stood up and the girls helped me into my cream high heels. A few minutes later, we entered the hotel ballroom. The music began, the guests stood up, and with my two best friends leading the way, I walked down the aisle to the man who loved me.

And with every step, I tried to forget about the man that I loved.

*   *   *

I watch from the back of the ballroom, as they say their

vows. The service is short and simple, though far more lavish than the registry office affair Marielle and I had in the parallel universe. I'm glad her angel had been able to create the illusion that the conversation we'd just had was merely a dream.

When I decided to ask her for another chance, I hadn't done so because I wanted to mess her around and ruin her wedding. I had asked because I needed to know there was no chance of us being together. So I can finally give up on the idea, and move on.

"Are you ready, Nathan?"

I look across at Marielle's guardian angel, who is also watching the service.

"Yes, I think I am. Will I meet my guardian angel now, when I cross over?"

The angel smiles at me. "You still haven't worked it out, have you? Nathan, I am your guardian angel."

"You? You're my guardian angel too?"

"Yes, I am."

"And that's why you were helping me? And why Marielle and I had such a strong bond?"

"Yes and yes. I'm sorry I never formally introduced myself."

"Wow. Thank you. For everything."

"It was my pleasure. And to answer your earlier question, you will meet other souls, but there are no angels there."

"Am I going to hell?"

My angel chuckles. "No, of course not. Such a place doesn't really exist. There are no angels there because no one needs helping or protecting. But should you decide to return to earth for another lifetime, you will be assigned another guardian angel to protect you."

"I see." I think for a while. The idea of moving on is

compelling, and the fact that I can return to earth in a new body and start over again is comforting. But somehow, it just doesn't feel right. "What if I don't want to move on, but I also don't want to stay here in spirit? What other options do I have?"

The angel is thoughtful for a while. "I guess you could parallel universe hop if you wanted to, but like I said before—"

"You need to find happiness where you are, and not go on a wild goose chase for it, I know, I know. I learned my lesson with that one, believe me."

The angel chuckles again. "What would you like to do?"

I think back to the parallel universe where I lost Marielle, and to the feeling I had when I held my baby girl in my arms. I'd allowed my grief and despair to take away the sheer joy and happiness I knew I could have had if I had chosen to stop chasing after a dream that was never to be. I know now, that I should never have left my baby girl.

"I know where I want to be, where I need to be," I say, as the happy couple walk past us down the aisle and out of the ballroom.

My angel smiles. "Say hello from me, and remind her that I am always there."

"I will."

I set my intention, and with the blessing of my angel, I close my eyes and return to her.

*　　　*　　　*

When I opened my eyes, the sun had fully risen in the sky, and I heard a noise behind me. I turned and walked over to the cot, where my little girl had woken up. I picked her up and cradled her in my arms until her cries quietened.

"Shh," I whispered. "It's okay, I'm here now. I'm here."

Thirty Years Later

I had missed Nathan every single day for the last thirty years.

Not that I wasn't very happy with Jack throughout that time, because I was. We had our challenges of course, but we always managed to get through them. We never had children, for some reason it just wasn't possible. I wasn't keen to try the fertility treatment route, and he didn't want to adopt. So it was just the two of us.

Until yesterday.

I looked around the bedroom, which seemed so big and empty without his presence. We had moved to a new house twenty years ago, after having one too many arguments about the cramped space in the cottage. I chose to rent the cottage out, rather than sell it. I guess despite all of my training and counselling others in letting go, there were still some things that I was unable to let go of.

The only comfort I had now was the fact that, thanks to Nathan, I knew that Jack would be okay. I knew the angels would take good care of him.

I sat on the edge of our bed, and touched the framed picture of us on our wedding day. We had shared a beautiful life together, and I wouldn't have changed it for the world. But the loss I felt now was tearing me to shreds.

"Jack?" I whispered into the empty room. "Are you there?"

But just like when I had called out for Nathan after our argument all those years ago, there was no response.

Six months passed by in a blur of funeral arrangements, dealing with tenants, selling the house and then moving. It brought back old memories of my father's funeral, and of leaving university. I wished I had someone to help me. Being back in the cottage made me miss both Nathan and Jack even more, but I could still see them both here, still feel their energies within the walls. And it was comforting.

One evening, alone in front of the fire to ward off the wintry chill, I decided to unpack some more of my books. I had considered, long ago, just giving them all to charity, as my interests had turned away from the metaphysical toward the psychological, and I had not touched any of the texts in years.

I got some scissors from the kitchen, slit open one of the boxes, and started pulling the books out in threes, placing them on the empty bookshelf. The fire popped suddenly, startling me and making me drop one of the books. I placed the other two on the shelf, and when I leaned down to pick up the copy of *Infinite You*, a note slid out.

Frowning, I picked the note up, and my heart thudded hard when I saw my name on the folded paper in a familiar cursive.

I sat down, and hands shaking, unfolded the paper.

My beautiful Marielle,

I am so sorry. I really cannot apologise enough for leaving you. But I need you to know the truth, the whole story, because without it, . you may not remember me with love, but instead with bitterness or resentment, and I could not stand it.

I did not leave you intentionally, I was trying to find a way to be with you. Properly. After reading this book, which suggests that we can choose to live in a parallel universe in which we can have all we desire, I spoke to your angel, and he confirmed that I could choose to live in a universe where I was still alive, and where we got to be together.

So that's what I did. I chose to live in a beautiful universe where I came and found you in university. A reality where you were able to say goodbye to your father, because I prompted you to contact him before it was too late. A life where we not only got married, but we had a beautiful child, and called her Snowdrop.

But there were flaws in this new universe that I chose, flaws that I had not thought to look for when I chose it. And so I chose to return to the universe where I was in spirit, so I could be with you again.

But I am too late. You are with Jack now, and you believe I abandoned you.

I will never be able to make it up to you, and for that, I am so very sorry. I hope you will have a very happy life with Jack, and I am going to do my very best to leave you be. Please know that I love you. Completely, absolutely, and for eternity. And I hope that you will one day forgive me.

Yours always,
Nathan.

His name smudged when my tears hit the bottom of the page. I looked at the date again. It was the day Jack had proposed to me. So he had been there, on the beach. Just like he had said in the weird dream I'd had of him on my wedding day.

And our child. Our life together. It hadn't just been vivid dreams. It had been real. Which meant that the reason he had left that universe was because I had died during childbirth.

All of the memories, half-memories and dreams slammed into me, leaving me breathless. I recalled sending him away, and for the first time in thirty years, felt a stab of regret.

What had I done?

The first sob surprised me, but more followed and soon I could no longer see the note, or the fire, or the world around me.

After what felt like hours, I felt a warmth fill me, and I knew I was not alone. "Jack?" I whispered. "Nathan?"

There was no answer, but I became very calm. My gaze rested on the book that had held Nathan's words all these years. Without fully thinking it through, I picked it up and flicked to a page with its corner folded down. It was a meditation to enter a parallel universe.

My breathing quickened, and I quickly re-read Nathan's words, then looked back at the book. If he had managed to choose another universe, one where we were together, then why couldn't I do the same thing? Surely there must be a universe where we are together, and we are happy, and neither of us dies young?

I breathed in deeply and carefully read the through the meditation a couple of times, committing it to memory so that I could do it with my eyes closed. Once I was sure I could remember the process, I closed my eyes.

*   *   *

When I woke up, I was confused. I didn't remember falling asleep. I rubbed my eyes and looked around. I wasn't on the sofa. I wasn't even in the cottage, I was—

"Marielle! If we're late one more time, I swear she's going to kill us!"

Suddenly wide awake, I leapt out of bed and all but ripped the door open. Sarah stared back at me, her young face expressing her shock. I threw my arms around her, and held her tight to me. In my parallel life, we had not seen each other for some time. After she had met her husband, they had emigrated to Australia and not returned to the UK, not even for holidays.

"Marielle?" Sarah squeaked. "Is everything okay?"

I could feel my tears soaking into her t-shirt, but I nodded. She pulled away from me a little and looked at me in concern.

"Are you sure?"

I nodded again, but was unable to speak. Suddenly, I remembered why I was there, and what I had just done. "What day is it? What's the date?"

Sarah frowned. "Why?"

I pulled away and ran into my room. I grabbed my phone from the bedside table and pushed the green button.

It was the day before Nathan was going to die.

Without even thinking, I grabbed yesterday's clothes from the floor, threw them on and shoved my feet into my shoes. I grabbed my car keys and went to the door, where Sarah was still standing, wearing the same expression of shock.

"Where are you going?"

"There's something I need to do," I said, pulling my door shut behind me and locking it. "Could you apologise for me not being in class today?"

Sarah nodded, but she didn't look happy.

"I'll explain it all later. But right now, I need to go." I headed out the front door of the dorm building, and crossed the car park to my old car. It struck me suddenly how amazing it felt to be in my young body again, how free and fit I felt. I unlocked the door and jammed the key into the ignition. Within seconds, I was pulling out of the front gates, and heading toward my old home town. Toward Nathan. I prayed that I would get there in time.

*　　*　　*

Feeling like a time traveler from the future, I walked down the high street, my heart thumping hard in my chest. If I had chosen right, I knew I would find Nathan at work.

I stepped into the shop, and glanced over at the checkout. An older woman was there, scanning someone's items. Refusing to believe that I might be too late, I headed further in, and started going up and down the aisles. It was near the tea that I finally saw his familiar outline.

Aware that tears were threatening to form and fall, I took a few deep breaths, before approaching him. He was so busy stacking the shelf, he wasn't aware of my presence. I cleared my throat gently.

"Excuse me, do you know where I can find the chocolate biscuits?"

He started to answer, but when he turned to look at me, his words died away. His eyes locked on mine, and I wondered if he was remembering the other universes, the other lifetimes.

"Marielle?" he whispered.

I smiled and took a step closer to him.

"I dreamed about you last night," he said, reaching out to touch my face. "It felt so real. And now here you are." He looked around him. "Is this a dream too?"

I moved closer still and then reached up to kiss him softly. He closed his eyes and kissed me back.

"This is real," I said. "It's not a dream. I'm here."

About the Author

Michelle lives in England, in the middle of the woods. When not writing and publishing her own books, she helps other Indie Authors with their own publishing adventures. She has known all her life that she is a writer. It is more of a calling than simply a passion, and despite her attempts to live in the normal world, she has finally realised that she would much rather live in a world full of magic and mystery.

Please feel free to write a review of this book on Amazon, or even just click the Like button. Michelle loves to get direct feedback, so if you would like to contact her, please e-mail theamethystangel@hotmail.co.uk or keep up to date by following her blog – **eata.wordpress.com.** You can also follow her on Twitter **@themiraclemuse** or 'like' her page on Facebook.

To sign up to her mailing list, visit:
www.michellegordon.co.uk

The Earth Angel Series:

The Earth Angel Training Academy (book 1)

Velvet is an Old Soul, and the Head of the Earth Angel Training Academy on the Other Side. Her mission is to train and send Angels, Faeries, Merpeople and Starpeople to Earth to Awaken the humans.

The dramatic shift in consciousness on Earth means that the Golden Age is now a possibility. But it will only happen if the Twin Flames are reunited, and the Indigo, Crystal and Rainbow Children come to Earth, to spread their love, light and wisdom.

While dealing with all the many changes, Velvet struggles to see the bigger picture. When she is reunited with her Flame for the first time in many lifetimes, her determination and resolve to fulfil her mission falter...

The Earth Angel Awakening (book 2)

'No matter how overcast the sky, the stars continue to shine. We just have to be patient enough to wait for clouds to lift.'

Twenty-five years after leaving the Earth Angel Training Academy to be born on Earth as a human, Velvet (now known on Earth as Violet) is beginning to Awaken.

But when she repeatedly ignores her dreams and intuition, she misses the opportunity to be with her Twin Flame, Laguz. Without the long-awaited reunion with her Twin Flame, can Violet possibly Awaken fully, and help to bring the world into the elusive Golden Age?

The Other Side
(of The Earth Angel Training Academy)

Mikey is an ordinary boy who just happens to talk to the Faeries at the bottom of his garden. So when an Angel visits him in his dream and tells him he must return to the Earth Angel Training Academy in order to save the world, despite his fears, he understands and accepts the task.

Starlight is the Angel of Destiny. By carefully orchestrating events at the Academy and on Earth, she can make sure that everything works out the way that it should, even though it may not make sense to those around her.

Leon is a Faerie Seer. He arrives at the Academy as a trainee, but through his visions he realises that his role in the Awakening is far more important than he ever imagined.

The Visionary Collection:

Heaven dot com

When Christina goes into hospital for the final time, and knows that she is about to lose her battle with cancer, she asks her boyfriend, James, to help her deliver messages to her family and friends after she has gone.

She also asks him to do something for her, but she dies before he can make it happen, and he finds it difficult to forgive himself.

After her death, her messages are received by her loved ones, and the impact her words have will change their lives forever.

The Doorway to PAM

When Natalie is rejected by the one that she has loved for more than ten years, she finds herself lost, lonely and in the middle of the woods. It is here, in the most unlikely place, that she finds PAM's Tearooms. Within this unusual place, as well as a sweet, strong cup of tea, Natalie also finds her purpose and herself.

She discovers that a whole dimension exists, that is only ever found by souls in despair. Run by a lady called Evelyn, who is supported by dreaming volunteers, it is in this dimension that souls who are lost, find the meaning in their lives once more.

It is here, that Natalie finds the love that she has been yearning for.

The Elphite

Ellie's life is just one long, bad case of déjà vu. She has lived her life before - a hundred times before - and she remembers each and every lifetime.

Each time, she has changed things, but has never managed to change the ending.

This time, in this life, she hopes that it will be different. So she makes the biggest change of all - she tries to avoid meeting him.

Her soulmate. The love of her life. Because maybe if they don't meet, she can finally change her destiny.

But fate has other ideas...

In gratitude for the nourishing vibrational
energy of the trees that have sustained me for
so many years, I have created:

Sacred Tree Spirit

In this dream-like space, you can
receive intergrated therapies, emotional
and core-belief re-programming and
vibrational healing.
You can relax in the mineral spa,
watch life-affirming films in our
imaginarium, attend courses and shop
for handmade gifts.
Or you could just come along for a
drink and a cake to meet like-minded
people.

sacred-tree-spirit.com

designs from a
different planet

madappledesigns
.co.uk

This book was published by The Amethyst Angel.

A selection of books bought to publication by The Amethyst Angel.
To view more of our published books visit **theamethystangel.com**

We have a selection of publishing packages available or we can tailor a package to suit each author's individual needs and budget. We also run workshops for groups and individuals on 'How to publish' your own books.

For more information on Independent publishing packages and workshops offered by The Amethyst Angel, please visit **theamethystangel.com**

Made in the USA
Charleston, SC
07 August 2014